FAREWELL TO THE KING

Farewell To The King

PIERRE SCHOENDOERFFER

TRANSLATED FROM THE FRENCH
BY XAN FIELDING

STEIN AND DAY/*Publishers*/*New York*

First published in English 1970
Copyright © 1970 in the English Translation
by William Collins Sons & Co., Ltd.
Copyright © Editions Bernard Grasset, 1969 as *L'adieu au Roi*
Designed by David Miller
Library of Congress Catalog Card No. 70-122424
Printed in the United States of America
Stein and Day/*Publishers*/7 East 48 Street, New York, N.Y. 10017
SBN 8128-1329-4

To Frédéric

Contents

"The homeland of a man who is
free to choose is where the biggest
clouds accumulate."

ANDRE MALRAUX

(The Walnut Trees of Altenburg)

PROLOGUE

1942

Freedom! To do what?

Big black clouds driven by the warm wind of the north-easterly monsoon scudded over the South China Sea. The swell built up into heavy leaden waves which smashed against the coast. The lifeboat creaked and grated as it grounded on the beach, then tipped over, spilling oars and survivors into the foaming surf.

It was February 13, 1942, a few days before the fall of Singapore.

The survivors were soldiers and sailors who had escaped from the city dying under Japanese bombs, their little coaster torpedoed and sunk in the night. Now, in the cold harsh light of dawn, they gazed at the gray sand on to which they had been cast by fate. Far to the east, the straw huts of a fishing village anchored in the dunes bowed before the driving rain. To the west, quite close, a dead tree, advance guard of a mighty forest, stood out against a cliff of dark jungle extending from the white line of surf and merging into the lowering sky.

A lieutenant—or was it a captain? no one seems to remember his name or rank—proposed taking a chance and heading for the village, waiting there until dark,

[13]

and persuading the fishermen to ship them all south-ward, to New Guinea and Australia, which the Japanese had not yet reached.

Chilled to the marrow and huddled together like sheep in the rain, the survivors argued for a moment. There was grumbling and swearing, even some show of resistance.

But this is all irrelevant now. Gradually, one after another, from exhaustion, from lassitude, they struggled painfully to their feet and set off toward the village.

One man alone did not move. He was a young, red-headed fellow with gray eyes, he wore an army uniform, and his torn battle-dress revealed an odd design tattooed on his chest: an eagle with wings outspread swooping on a dragon.

He was cleaning the breech of his rifle, clogged with sand and salt. He did not look up until the officer, with a shrug, had walked away in his turn to join the group heading for the village in the rain. Then, turning his back on him, the man with gray eyes set off toward the dead tree and the forest, walking through the surf so that the sea would wash out his footprints.

All but one of those who followed the officer were killed or died of exhaustion in Japanese prison camps. The sole survivor, a sailor, managed one night to steal a fishing prahu, in which he took four months to reach Australia. He was no doubt the last white man to leave Borneo.

He recalls that the man with gray eyes had an argument with the officer. He even vaguely remembers that the man spoke of freedom and said something like,

[14]

"Now we're free, sir, free to go our own ways." Or perhaps he had merely said, "Now I'm free."

This is not of much importance either, because the great island of Borneo was about to sink into Japanese obscurity. For four years it was to disappear from the eyes of the West, as though it had been wiped off the map of the world.

PART ONE

The
Northeasterly
Monsoon

"For myself, I see no middle course:
this man must either reign or die!"

SAINT-JUST

(Speech on the Death of the King)

I was the first white man to see Learoyd again, and I ought to have killed him on the spot. I would have saved the King of England a great deal of trouble. But I did not know at the time that he was already mad, wild like an old rogue elephant, amuck like a Malay pirate. Subsequently I became friends with Learoyd, the mad king.

At the beginning of 1945 General MacArthur, when planning the recapture of the Philippines ("I shall return!"), decided on an "invasion" of Borneo to cover his left flank. The British then thought of infiltrating some special agents into the country to find out what was happening and to organize an uprising in support of this landing. That is why, after several grim weeks of training in Australia, I found myself, festooned with weapons and parachutes, in the fuselage of a four-engine American Liberator. I had been selected because in 1936 I had taken part in a three months' expedition among the head-hunters, as a botanist. Special Forces were not exactly rich in men with a knowledge of the interior of Borneo.

The prospect of returning there had appealed to me;

I was only too pleased to leave Darwin and the quick-sand of the training camp. I had been made a captain and my radio operator was Sergeant Anderson, a swarthy little Australian who had been through Tobruk.

The Liberator was flying above clouds as dark as the sea, from which almost pitch-black, jungle-clad mountains emerged. On our right rose the huge jagged bulk of Mount Kinabalu, which, despite the altitude of the aircraft, still towered above us from its fourteen thousand feet. I had expended all my energy on the departure; now I felt drained and miserable and kept asking myself, "Why?" Luckily a parachute jump requires no initiative; it's a passive action. You topple out and that's that.

There is nothing very unusual about all this, I know. Men were dropped all over Asia during the last war—and even afterward—and all of them felt their hearts contract a bit. Some of them foundered, leaving no more trace in the jungle than a submarine in deep water. Others came back emaciated and wrote books—some bad, some outstanding—about their experiences. But I don't want to tell you about my war, as my father told me about his. All these wars are always drearily alike: you tramp through mud, you wait for hours, you open fire, they fall. That is how war seems when you get back. But the wind has swept away the stench of the corpses, and all we remember is the flare of our youth.

No! What I want to tell you is the story of the last king of Borneo.

For most of you Borneo doesn't exist. It's an imaginary setting like Tibet or Tierra del Fuego, distant in space and remote in time. But I know the island exists, because it was there that I discovered a new variety of Nepenthes, a pitcher plant, sometimes erroneously called a carnivorous orchid—and because it was there, deep in the dark forest of the Muruts' territory, that I came across the red king with the gray eyes. But I am anticipating.

I landed in a swamp of green mud, into which I sank up to the waist. A few seconds later Anderson vanished from sight behind some bushes, and I heard him grumbling as he floundered about like a buffalo. The equipment container drifted down more slowly, and its parachute caught in the tall trees growing all around the hollow. The Liberator had disappeared, but we could still hear the diminishing roar of its engines through the shrill grating sound of the insects.

There we were, the first white men to return to this part of Borneo since the Japanese invasion: a botanist, formerly a lecturer at Reading University and now a temporary captain in the British Army, and a swarthy little Australian who had probably been a sheep breeder somewhere in Queensland.

The vast, still forest surrounded us on all sides, a splendid evergreen forest in which I could already discern a few *Antiaris toxicaria* and a lovely specimen of *Fraycinetia lianoides*. The terrain bore no resemblance to the aerial photographs of the drop zone which I had been given to study in the camp, and I wondered if the navigator, unable to find it in the clouds, had not simply tipped us out at random. All I knew was that we must

[21]

be somewhere in Murut territory (unless the navigator had done something stupid) in a little valley of one of the tributaries of the great Sambakung River.

Anderson cocked his Tommy gun and sent mud flying in all directions as he dragged himself out of the swamp and struggled over toward me. A hundred yards away, on a little mound near the edge of the forest, an almost naked man had just appeared. He stood there watching us, leaning nonchalantly on his spear like a Greek warrior.

In Darwin I had read all the available material on the native populations of Borneo. It did not amount to much. The Chartered Company, which had administered the State of Sabah in North Borneo since 1881, had kept its archives at Sandakan, the capital, and they were now in Japanese hands. In any case the Company had shown less interest in the tribes of the interior, who were fairly inaccessible, than in the former Malay pirates on the coast. During my 1936 expedition we had in fact made good use of a few hillmen as porters, but they were directed by an educated native who spoke Malay, and I had had hardly any contact with them.

The Muruts, like the Mois of Indochina and the Sakais of Malaya, are a race whose origins are obscure. Fiercely independent, they are economically self-sufficient and band together in villages consisting of a single longhouse capable of accommodating several hundred families. They grow mountain rice and hunt wild animals with poisoned darts. Their only contact with the outside world is due to the vital necessity of obtaining salt from the coast (we had several sacks of salt in our

[22]

container). Finally, they were said to have given up head-hunting a couple of generations ago.

It was starting to rain by the time we joined our warrior. He had a lithe, muscular body, and the rain accentuated the bronze of his skin, which was polished smooth like a pebble. I at once asked him the question that was worrying me:

"Japanese? Nippons? Nippons?"

He appeared not to understand. I persisted, pointing at the ridges around us.

"Nippons? Nippons?"

"Bah!" he replied.

Anderson lit him a cigarette, which he accepted with pleasure, shielding it from the downpour under the palm of his hand.

I pointed my finger at his chest and tried another tack.

"Muruts? Muruts?"

"Bah!"

I had known all along that we would have some difficulty in making ourselves understood, but this armed character with his warrior-like manner made me uneasy. He could easily belong to a Japanese auxiliary patrol. He drew on his cigarette with satisfaction and said something that sounded like "Comanches!"

Anderson tapped him on the chest.

"Comanches?"

The warrior started laughing and gleefully repeated, "Comanches, Comanches."

"He's a Comanche, sir," Anderson translated. "He says he's a Comanche."

[23]

The conversation was becoming absurd. Other warriors emerged silently from the forest, and it appeared that they were all Comanches. One of them, who seemed to be the headman and wore a head-hunter's sword at his waist, its sheath adorned with long black fringes resembling scalps, suddenly declared, "You, come with me."

He spoke English, English with a jarring accent but quite comprehensible. Anderson triumphantly confirmed the fact: "He speaks English, he speaks English."

Once I had got over my surprise, the first thing I wanted to find out was whether there were any Japanese in the neighborhood; second, if these people were prepared to help us. From the confused replies, half in broken English, half in Murut dialect, it appeared that no, the Japanese were nowhere near, and yes, they were going to help us, they were even going to guide us to another valley, one day's march away, where there was a village and a chieftain: a white man like us, a man who spoke English like us.

One of the objectives of my mission, apart from organizing resistance activity, was to contact any white men who might be hiding out in the jungle: crews of downed aircraft, escaped prisoners, or surviving members of the Company staff. So everything was turning out for the best. The Muruts undertook to recover the parachutes and container, and still in pelting rain, we plunged into the jungle.

Before nightfall the chief with the head-hunter's sword halted our column and organized a temporary camp. I was chilled to the marrow but very happy. In

[24]

the gleam of the fire which had been kindled to cook our rice, I made a few notes on some serrated orchids *(cypripedies)* I had collected on the track. In that slightly euphoric state of inebriation which comes from exhaustion, I felt that my sojourn in Borneo had got off to a good start and that it offered me, moreover, a splendid opportunity to complete my 1936 report on the flora of equatorial Asia. I even envisaged compiling a little herbarium for Kew Gardens.

Although it had stopped raining the warriors had built us a small straw shelter, but Anderson and I preferred to sling our hammocks between a couple of trees, as we had been taught in the camp at Darwin. To salve my conscience, I arranged a system of sentry duty with him before falling asleep like a log.

A nip in the air heralded the dawn. I felt snug and warm in my hammock, but I was unable to move a muscle. Anderson gave a yell, then I heard him struggling and swearing abominably.

I was trussed up in my hammock. At first I thought it was a nightmare, but two of the Murut warriors attached me to a long bamboo pole, hoisted me to their shoulders, and set off.

Slowly the sky grew lighter, a great gust of wind shook the forest, and yesterday's deluge began again worse than ever. Rain in England has something gentle and slightly melancholy about it, but here it is a steady battering, heavy, vertical, frightening—a primitive, pitiless force that seems incapable of stopping. Helpless, jolted at every step, I was blinded by the streams of rain

[25]

which slid down my clothing like icy reptiles. Creepers as limp and clammy as octopus tentacles lapped at my face, and I kept envisaging the leeches.

Hour after hour the Murut warriors pursued their silent, springy progress. From time to time an unexpected series of jolts told me that a fresh porter was taking over under the bamboo yoke; occasionally a barely perceptible slackening in the pace would give the leading man time to hack a breach in the rampart of tangled vegetation. Then the regular rocking motion would resume. Benumbed, I lost all sense of time.

All of a sudden I was flung to the ground, my nose and mouth in the mud. I jerked on to my back to avoid suffocating, and it was then I saw Learoyd. He was standing in front of me, gaunt and almost naked, head and shoulders taller than the horde of warriors whose bodies glistened under the cataracts of rain. His long red hair was plastered against his forehead like seaweed. His eyes were gray. An eagle swooping on a dragon was tattooed on his chest.

He took my American carbine which the headman handed to him and examined its mechanism intently, then he said something in Murut and my porters cut the parachute rigging-lines which bound me in the hammock. I tried to get up: my cramped muscles refused to respond and I remained crouching, trembling in the mud like a beast at bay. I was fuming with rage. Learoyd tossed my weapon over to me, and I eventually managed to struggle to my feet. His pale eyes were fixed on me, eyes as cold and gray as winter. I think I could have killed him, I think that between his life and his death there was at that moment no more than the thickness of a cigarette paper.

Anderson in his turn rose to his feet and took a few uncertain steps, rubbing his arms to restore the circulation. The circle of naked warriors had closed in on us. They were not menacing, merely watchful. I was still in a raging temper, furious at having felt frightened, furious at having been made a fool of, furious at being weak, covered in mud, soaking wet . . . and the infernal rain which had not stopped since dawn! I knew even before he opened his mouth that it was this white man with the red hair who had engineered this reception, who had ordered the Muruts to trap us and fling us at his feet like dogs or slaves. But who was this man and what did he want? I was still trembling and I had to make an effort to ask in a voice that I should have liked to be calm and chilly, but which to my own ears sounded like a whimper, "Why did you do this?"

"If I had demanded it they wouldn't have brought anything but your heads."

Learoyd gave the ghost of a smile as he watched my reaction, and when I remained as icy as before, he openly burst out laughing. A surge of hilarity stirred the warriors round us. They had surely not understood a word, but they were laughing with absolute confidence.

"This is my home ground."

Learoyd was no longer laughing, and his face had become inscrutable.

"I'm master here and I want everyone to know it."

Gray eyes are peculiar in that they betray no emotion, and in its absence one cannot help imagining a

[27]

world of violence and passion behind their gaze. But this time I did not need to imagine: the passion was there, pure as a diamond, and even my fury melted in its blaze. Suddenly I had the impression that he, not I, was the beast at bay, and he was reacting like a beast making a stand. His instinct warned him of danger. Behind me he sensed vast anonymous powers. One thing was certain: by some strange accident this half-naked man had become master here. And he intended to remain so.

I am trying to recollect this moment exactly, head in hands and eyes closed. It is so long ago, already almost twenty-five years ago. I was a young dog in those days and I must have barked like a young dog. Learoyd—but I did not yet know his name and had no idea of his astonishing story—stood unmoving, with his pack of savage warriors gathered around him in the pelting rain. For the first time (or was it later, when we were walking to the village?) I noticed some military weapons among the blowpipes and head-hunter's swords: Ichikawa rifles and a Japanese machine gun of the sort we were shown in training.

The rain stopped as abruptly as it had started at dawn that morning, and a merciless sun thrust between the trees through a break in the black clouds. The forest was steeped in a dank hothouse atmosphere reeking of fermentation, teeming with life, so that one almost expected to see this primeval vegetation sprout and swell like those flowers whose monstrous blossoming is revealed at an accelerated speed in laboratory films.

[28]

The jungle is terrible like the sea, it is a tempestuous swell whose inert power seems even more forbidding. One solitary tree standing upright, defying gravity, already represents a challenge, a miracle of life on the weight of the world. But the jungle is a luxuriance which creeps, clings, clambers, clutches, strangles and kills in its boa-constrictor embrace, a monster which plunges roots into the putrefaction of death to hoist itself still higher in an aggressive quest for the warmth of God.

One day when I was a child, my father took me to see a pink granite quarry in Wales. He showed me how the rock could be split by means of little wedges of damp wood. The memory of this probably determined my vocation as a botanist: so much invisible power in a tiny piece of wood had fascinated me.

I don't remember what I replied to Learoyd. I had pins and needles in my legs as the circulation got going again and I thought I felt the ruthless jungle vitality boiling within me. I was on a mission; I was determined to carry it out and not let myself be led by this visionary. The master, the proconsul, if there had to be one, would be me. I should have to be careful, however, and not cross swords with Learoyd until I was firmly entrenched in the country. Afterward I would manage somehow to eliminate him, evacuate him to Darwin as soon as communications were possible. Time was on my side; meanwhile I needed to establish a temporary balance of power.

I had to clear my throat in order to steady my voice and assume the slightly standoffish Guards-officer tone (which would have delighted my instructor) in which I explained that the Japanese had lost the war, that Australian troops would be landing shortly to recapture—I mean liberate—this country (a significant slip), and that I was entrusted with the task of organizing this liberation:

"The wind has veered to the west and everything is reverting to normal. The British will be back. That's how things stand and there's nothing you can do to change the situation."

My speech must have been somewhat over-simple and conventional, but I had boundless self-confidence in those days. As I said before, I was a young dog then and I barked like a young dog. The wind was never going to veer to the west, apart from a mild breeze in the backwash of the Japanese defeat. The wind was in the east, once and for all, but few people realized it at the time.

Learoyd did not move immediately; he remained silent, inscrutable, and his expression gave no hint of what he was thinking. Then he issued a few orders in Murut and gradually his warriors slipped off through the trees of the forest toward the village. Anderson was supervising the porters as they loaded up the empty hammocks, parachutes, and container. As he passed me he whispered:

"Who's this character? He's round the bend!"

The village was situated on the slope of a denuded hill. It consisted of a single longhouse built on piles. It could accommodate a thousand people. Some dogs were barking, and we sensed a multitude of dark eyes watching us through the gaps in the bamboo walls. Learoyd, still not uttering a word, installed us under a sort of veranda earmarked for visiting bachelors. Anderson and I undressed and went down, wrapped in sarongs, to bathe in the torrent flowing among the vegetable patches at the foot of the hill. It was a marvelous moment of sheer physical delight which washed away our last remnants of anger. The water was so cool, and the sun so hot, that we kept plunging in and out, much as one turns this way and that in front of a blazing log fire on a spring night in England. A few children had followed us and the more inquisitive ones presently drew closer, their little golden froglike bodies wriggling in the spray of the current. Anderson showed them how to skip rocks with some flat pebbles, and they almost split their sides laughing when he patiently tried to teach them the words "Good morning, sir."

Some women, from a safe distance on the bank, kept up a running commentary on our activities and from time to time called out to admonish one or another of the cheekier brats. I lit a cigarette and we went back, feeling ravenously hungry, pursued by a shrill chorus of "Good morning, sir! Good morning, sir!"

Learoyd was waiting for us in the warm penumbra of the veranda, surrounded by some of his warriors, including the headman who spoke English and who had tied us up so firmly in our hammocks during the night. The women had prepared some manioc and pork, and there was a jar, decorated with a dragon, full of ayak, a rice wine. We joked together as we ate and drank; I

[31]

wanted to win them over before putting my questions to them.

And suddenly Learoyd spoke.

He went on speaking for hours; long after night had fallen I was still listening to him. Anderson, who had started unpacking the transmitter and our equipment from the container, stopped. It was a monologue, one of those long conversations one carries on with oneself. It was a halt after a long march, when a man turns around to contemplate the distance he has covered and finds in that contemplation added reasons for continuing and fresh strength to struggle on. The amount of ayak he drank played no part in his need to express himself.

Learoyd began in a detached laconic fashion, with numerous detours to try to avoid the steepest line of approach, but as he went on I felt increasingly how overburdened he was.

I shall make no attempt to transcribe his exact words. His vocabulary was poor and he could no longer construct a sentence properly; one had to detect his train of thought from disconnected phrases, silences, hesitations, to decipher it from the tone of his voice.

"When I arrived at this house I was almost dead, I was dead. They had dumped me right here; it's a place reserved for unmarried men on the move from other tribes. They were deliberating whether to hand me over to the Japanese whole or merely my head. But I didn't yet know this because, as I say, I was almost dead. Besides, I didn't understand the language. I have had to learn their language like a child learning how to talk, because they didn't know a word of English either. It was I who taught it to Ballang Gwai, my brother, that man over there who brought you to me.

"The Japanese were emphatic. Any white man had to be handed over dead or alive. Otherwise . . . Only they were far away, twenty days' march to the west. I was too weak to be handed over at once, and the village headman, Gwai's father, didn't want my head cut off.

"He knew something about white men. He had spent two years in prison at Keningau before the war. He had caught a madman, a cook or gardener who had gone beserk and dashed off into the forest with a bottle of whisky belonging to the District Commissioner. This had caused quite a stir. Gwai's father was roaming around to buy some salt; he came upon the madman quietly drinking his whisky, propped up against a tree in the forest. That evening he called on the District Commissioner, who was sitting out on the veranda with his wife, and restored to him not only the bottle of whisky, which was still half full, but also the head of his cook. The lady of the house gave a piercing shriek and fell down in a faint. She was pregnant, according to Gwai's father. That's how he discovered that head-hunting had become a thing of the past.

That's probably what saved me, that white woman's shriek and the two years in prison that followed, which had left Gwai's father with pleasant memories. I was almost dead, they would have cut off my head without my even noticing; and when I began to get better I used to howl all night as though I was fighting against the devil himself. They became frightened then, thinking I was fighting off an evil spirit, fighting against this dragon I had had tattooed on my chest in Penang. But let me tell you something—what I was fighting against was the jungle."

Learoyd fell silent for some time, absorbed in his memories, then he said something to Ballang Gwai and took a few mouthfuls of ayak. His face brightened when a little boy came toddling up to him and wedged himself between his thighs. He was as chubby and tanned as the ones who had played with us in the torrent, but I saw that his eyes, which observed us intently, were gray.

"This is my son," Learoyd announced proudly. "A regular little Comanche."

"A Comanche?" I echoed.

"That's what I call them. At Penang, at the beginning of the war, I saw an American film, *The White Comanche*. I forgot to tell you I was stationed in Malaya, at Penang—a sergeant in the Argylls. My name is Learoyd, Sergeant Learoyd. It was a very good film, I saw it twice—a little white boy, kidnapped by the Indians, who becomes a Comanche chief. The end was bad, he fell in love with a girl, a white girl, and she insisted on his toeing the line and becoming a cowboy like everyone else. He didn't want to. In the end she got her way in spite of everything, and it's sad, because he betrayed his brothers, the Comanches. All the same, the beginning was good. I often thought of it. The people here look rather like Red Indians, don't you think? So I called them my Comanches, and when I organized my little army they became the Comanches, just like that.

"His mother is Gwai's sister, she's of noble lineage, descendant of Paang, the hero who tamed fire in ancient times. She's my wife, I married her when I was beginning to speak a little, after the duel with Lian the Magnificent. It was she who really taught me their language. It's easier with a woman. I've learned a lot from the women. The men here dream of God. They'd cut your throat as soon as look at you. The headmen—the sages with ears full of wisdom, they call them—spend half the night drinking. They want to rival the heroes of the days of high adventure. So there's nothing to be got out of them, they just strike noble attitudes. For them it's man that counts, not life.

"The women are simpler, more flexible, they're a

[35]

tireless flow of life. They're the ones who saved me. They're curious, I intrigued them, my eyes intrigued them, they said I had eyes like the sea. They don't know the sea back here, but it's very important because the sea means salt. They also used to say: 'Is your heart good? Is your heart bad? Your eyes say nothing. They are like two stones in the sunshine or in the rain.'

"I delivered my son myself with my own hands. It lasted a whole night and they were all muttering around me, in an ugly mood, because I wasn't following the custom. A year earlier they would have killed me for that, or driven me out. But by this time I was sufficiently powerful and they no longer dared. It was my own son, you understand? He was of my blood and of my people's blood, I wasn't going to leave it to them. It lasted a whole night, in the forest, in front of a big bonfire, and I was frightened she might die. But this little rascal wanted to live, and I fished him out all red and blood-stained just as the sun was rising.

"There were some Japanese on the prowl in the area. They had already burned down Senghir's longhouse, two days' march to the west, because he refused to pay the rice tax. They were also looking for me. Later on, with Gwai and a few others, we wiped out one of their patrols—the whole patrol—in one night. It just vanished. Not a man got back to tell the tale. The Japanese never knew what had happened. We collected the weapons. That was the start of the Comanches.

"The Japanese stayed for a long time. Eventually, at the start of the heavy rains of the northeasterly monsoon, they moved down to the coast because a Chinese, Doctor

Kwok, had organized an uprising.* We were left in peace for quite a time. This was in 1943, October 1943. We came back to the longhouse, which had not been burned, and for the whole of one moon we made sacrifices to purify ourselves because we had hidden in the Forest of the Spirits.

"I ought to explain, we are in the Spirit country. My people are the sons of the First Man, living in the domain of the Spirits. There are three sorts of forest. The Forest of the Spirits, the Forest for Hunting, and lastly the Forest for Eating, for burning down and growing rice. It's the law of the ancients. There's a saying that applies to the whole territory"—Learoyd recited it in Murut before translating it for my benefit—

> Forest of the Spirits: Man, beware of the law.
> Forest for Hunting: Man, beware of the law.
> Forest for Growing Rice: Man, thou art free.

"I had infringed the law by having my son born in the Forest of the Spirits, but there were the heads of the Japanese soldiers for the sacrifices, and everyone here thinks I have a special relationship with the spirits because—maybe because of the duel as well—because when I was almost dead I used to howl and struggle every night. They believed my twin souls were fighting against the demons."

* Known from its date, 10/10/43, as "The Double Tenth." Dr. Kwok and his "Kinabalu Guerrillas" seized the port of Jesselton on the west coast to prepare for a rumored American landing. The Japanese reprisals were unbelievably brutal and lasted six months. Nearly three thousand Malays and Chinese died of starvation and over a thousand were shot or beheaded.

Once again Learoyd was at a loss for words. He remained silent and strangely still, as tense as an animal on the alert, ready to take flight. His gray eyes were vacant, more fathomless than ever. The women were right: those eyes of his said nothing.

"Demons! Monsters! Ha! Ha!"—he laughed bitterly —"No! I was fighting against the jungle. Afterward I was covered in boils and abscesses, as though the devil was drawing the madness from my flesh.

"Have you ever spent a night out in the jungle? All alone? I have . . . No, I don't want to talk about it."

Later on he did talk about it all the same, as one fingers the edges of a wound that aches. The time had not yet come. The sun was only just beginning to disappear behind the heights, setting Learoyd's red locks aflame. We had to wait until nightfall and drink still more ayak.

"You've come too late. If I had waited for you, I'd be dead—I knew you were going to come back, I knew it all along, but it's too late—either dead or raving mad. I'm no longer one of you.

"No white man has ever set foot in this territory. Never, before me. And I ought to have died ten times over, I ought never to have got here. I'm an animal that's hard to kill. I went through the whole withdrawal in Malaya, from the Grik Road north of Perak right down to the bottom. Taiping and the Battle of the River Slim. Our captain used to say, I remember, 'If I think you're alive, I think of you marching. So march, keep marching.' He was killed on the Slim.

"Keep marching! To get here, I had to drag myself along on my belly like a worm, beseeching God to . . . It's too deep in the interior, here; the jungle is too dense, too difficult. Besides, they don't want anyone, they don't need anyone. Some Malays and Chinese who tried to open up trading posts—their skulls are still here. Some white men, too, Englishmen in the early colonial days, if I understand the heroic songs of the days of high adventure. And even a Dutchman, not so long ago, staying with that old rogue Tamong Miri.

"No, they don't want anyone. They are the free people, the sons of the First Man in the Domain of the Spirits. To hell with the rest of the world! They have everything here, there's nothing they need."

"What about salt?" Remembering the documents I had read at Darwin, I interrupted Learoyd. "You need salt from the coast, so do they."

"Yes, that's true, salt! Of course! If you travel twenty days up north or westward to the sea, you'll come across squalid villages and groveling men dressed in shabby Malayan clothes. They're the same race as the people here, but if you ask them which tribe they belong to, they don't know. If you ask them who they are, who their ancestors were, who their great headmen were, they don't know. If you ask them who owns the land on which they live, they don't know. They are the Red Dogs, the sacrificed tribes. Their role in life is to establish contacts with the exterior, first with the Chinese and Malays, then with the English, now with the Japanese. It's from them we get our salt, the iron for our swords,

[39]

the echo of the sound and fury of the outside world. They are losing their own souls, but they are saving ours. That's how it is.

"When I first arrived they didn't want me here. I was as weak as a newborn babe. They palavered every night, while I kept howling, to see how they were going to get rid of me. And then I started to live again. Like a child, I learned to walk, I learned to talk. It's the women who brought me up, like a child, as I told you—I might as well have been suckled by them.

"A relative of Gwai's—his cousin, a warrior, a noble, Lian the Magnificent—was all for handing me over to the Japanese. Every night I used to listen to this fire-eater holding forth, though I couldn't understand a word he said. He wanted my hide—well, actually only my head, because the nearest Japanese outpost was at Tomani, which was too far to carry me intact. He had finally convinced the others.

"Then Gwai's sister, Yoo, who was to become my wife, hid me in the forest, spending every night with me to stop my howling. One evening, when I was able to speak a little, I went to the council. I said, 'If Lian the Magnificent wants my head, he must come and get it. If he wants to slice it off with a head-hunter's sword, I shall defend myself with a head-hunter's sword.' I said, 'This is only fair. If Lian the Magnificent is a warrior, I too am a warrior. If he is noble, how does he know that I too am not noble?' I said, 'Lian the Magnificent and I drink the same water, live off the same forest. Our great ancestors say fairly, we have the same rights.'

"I said all this as best I could. I must have made

[40]

some mistakes, but no one laughed. I sat down and drank some ayak from the jar. Gwai's father—he has since died —was then headman and answerable for the unwritten law. Gwai's father replied, 'This is only fair.'

"I fought against Lian the Magnificent and I killed him.

"He was a great warrior. I—but I've already told you the condition I was in.

"In my lifetime the English have taught me two things. I'm an Irishman, and I owe this to them—two things, two useful things. Bayonet fighting, and the history of the kings of England in the Middle Ages. Yes, the history of the kings of England, how they rallied the feudal dukes and barons to the Crown. That came in useful later on, when I organized the Comanche army.

"Lian the Magnificent wounded me seven times, but I believe he was frightened of my eyes. Suddenly he fell, and he said, 'I'm dying. The red man with the gray eyes has killed me.' Blood was flowing from his right side like a river. I went down to the torrent to bathe my wounds and clean my sword. When I got back he was dead.

"No one said anything more about cutting off my head. I married. Gwai became my brother, and I was entitled to sit at the council. I went on learning the language. It's a language that has never been written down. Everything—the laws, customs, legal declarations, the legends of the days of high adventure, the poems to the glory of the dead chieftains—everything is memorized. I had to invent a way to write it down because I couldn't remember everything. I transcribed into English the sounds I heard, and I invented various accents,

[41]

because many similar sounds have a different meaning. After the first Japanese reprisals I organized a school where the children could learn to read and write, but I was not successful with the adults. Even English they can't manage, except for Gwai.

"When we got back to the longhouse after the birth of my son and the departure of the Japanese, Gwai's father died. The whole village gathered on the big mountain overlooking the Plain of Elephants in the east. Others came from far off, from the Red Lands, with those of Senghir's men who had escaped the Japanese massacre, others from further off still, from the Black Lands, four or five days' march away, to take part in the sacrifice of the seven buffaloes and seven jars, for Gwai's father was a great headman.

"On the third night I spoke. I said,

" 'I am Learoyd. Alone I killed Lian the Magnificent in single combat, and I am sad because he was a noble warrior. I am the husband of the headman's daughter, the descendant of Paang who tamed fire in ancient times. I am the brother of Ballang Gwai. You know all this but I am repeating it so that no one shall say, this man is a stranger.

" 'Now listen to me. You were a great free people, the people of the Three Forests, and strangers used to tremble with fear at the mere sound of your name! To-day you are like the Red Dogs, and the stranger strides over your land, burns down your houses—remember, Senghir—molests your women—remember that Japanese officer who demanded a fresh girl every night. He takes your buffaloes and your pigs and gives you nothing in exchange. He steals your rice. He hunts in the Forest of the Spirits. Remember, O Senghir, remember.

" 'The law, handed down by your ancestors for a thousand generations, says that no stranger must be allowed to enter your territory. The law says this, does it not? You reply, they have formidable weapons and we have none. But I tell you the Japanese soldiers are not invincible. They make as much noise moving along a trail as a herd of elephants, they are unable to read the land so as to avoid the snares, and they are afraid of the demons of darkness.

" 'Remember, Gwai my brother, and you, the Comanches—did we not kill seventeen of them in one night? Did we not capture seventeen formidable weapons in one night? The Japanese have gone, but they will come back. You must believe me because I know yesterday, today, and tomorrow. Each village must raise a troop of warriors, as we did with Gwai. All these troops must obey a single headman and train in warfare. Then we shall once again be the great free people.

" 'The war gongs will sound in the mountains, and our enemies, who are accustomed to our slumbering, will say, it's only thunder. The warriors will brandish their weapons, glittering in the sunlight, and our enemies will say, it's only lightning. The warriors will pour down into the valley and our enemies will say, it's only rain. Like tigers on the prowl, the warriors will fire their poisoned arrows from their blowpipes and our enemies will say, it's only flies buzzing. When they realize their mistake it will be too late.'

"That is how I spoke on the third night. It was a fine

[43]

speech, inspired by the great epic poems of the days of high adventure. I had rehearsed it with Yoo, and even Gwai didn't know of it. Before dawn, by the gleam of the dying embers, I knew I had won. I told you, man dreams of God. But one still has to find words to fire his imagination. I had spent a whole year learning the words."

Several dragon jars had been brought in, and the ayak gradually went to our heads in the muggy atmosphere of the veranda. Young girls with bare breasts sat smoking their pipes, wavering in the flickering light of torches, and behind them, in the shadows beyond, were the blinking eyes of the newcomers who kept turning up, to drink and to observe us. Some of the warriors had passed out where they sat and were snoring gently; others, their faces glistening with sweat, rose unsteadily to their feet and staggered out into darkness in which gleamed the green eyes of the dogs kept tethered at a distance. Peals of laughter, hoarse cries rose above the constant murmur of voices, and every so often the bamboo structure would creak like the rigging of an old vessel lying at anchor.

The little boy with the gray eyes had toddled off again, belly thrust forward, just as he had come. Learoyd sat facing the light, with his back to the darkness of the jungle, whose tallest trees stood faintly outlined against the starlit sky. He had drunk a great deal but did not seem intoxicated, although his self-control was slipping and he was certainly talking more than he had intended. He still stumbled over his words, but I had the feeling that he was gradually recovering his vocabulary, that he was now glad to be speaking English, that he was captivated by the magic of speech. I thought of those taciturn old sea captains, sole masters on board after God, who one evening, in a grimy bar miles away from the ocean, suddenly blurt out the story of their lives.

I had many questions to ask him, but I preferred not to interrupt the flow of this great underground river which an accident had brought out into the open, for fear of its disappearing again. I would have time tomorrow to find out exactly where we were and where the Japanese were, while Anderson tried to contact Darwin via Morotai, the American advance base in the Halmaheras.

Learoyd had stopped, as though reluctant to continue; his eyes were fixed on me, but I had the unpleasant sensation that he was looking straight through me and seeking something farther off. I was surprised when he went on again in a steady voice:

"Yes, a leader must always be a poet. He must speak in the name of the gods, of the spirits, and the spirits of the dead. For these people who cannot write, words are like fire. I could feel them gradually glowing, coming to life. Soon they were burning, dreaming. Everything I told them that night, I believed. Except about Lian. As you can imagine, I wasn't sad at all. The beast had almost put an end to me.

"It's like the Middle Ages here, each tribal chief is a little feudal baron. It was time for the barons to unite if they wanted to survive, but no one of them was strong enough to impose his law on the others. I was creating an army, and I claimed I was reviving the glory of the days of high adventure. An army is not enough to make a kingdom, but at least it's a start. That scrawny old crow Senghir and the other headmen present were well aware of this, and they were frightened of seeing their power diminished. Especially Senghir.

"The army! It would never give battle as I had told them. No! I had thought it over for a long time. There was no question of defeating the Japanese, only of making their stay here as unpleasant as possible and, with a bit of luck, wiping out any small unit that ventured too far. My idea was for each village to raise and maintain a militia to guard its own sector of territory. In case of trouble it would summon all the other militias to its aid and organize resistance. I wanted to appoint each militiaman, each Comanche, myself, so as to know them all personally. I wanted to organize their training, and above all I wanted to hand over ceremonially one of the weapons taken from the Japanese patrol, complete with a palaver, ayak, sacrifices to the spirits, the lot.

"I was dispersing my armament, but it was to my advantage. In any case my armament didn't amount to much: one machine gun, fifteen rifles, and one revolver. The ammunition situation was even worse—fifty rounds per rifle and four belts for the machine gun. There was another, even greater weakness. Salt. If the Japanese thought of cutting off the salt supply and preventing us from getting it from the Red Dogs, the revolt would fizzle out in three months. In this place, salt means life.

[47]

"I picked up my stick and, with Gwai and a few of the original Comanches, set out on a tour of the villages. First of all I had to win over the local headman, then put the militia on a proper footing and start instruction. They knew nothing, not even how to use the sights of a rifle: each time I expended half the ammunition available for the weapon, but by this means I inspired the young ones.

"Yet I was getting nowhere. I was floundering in a swamp without being able to set foot on firm ground. It was only when the Tamong Miri business was settled that things looked up. You must realize, long-standing quarrels, grisly blood feuds poison relations between tribes. As the saying goes,

> Fish of the same river devour one another.
> Sons born of the same woman slay one another.

"Half the villages were prepared to fall on the other half with anything at hand. Civil war was always simmering, so you can imagine that with rifles . . . To try to create an army, I first of all had to wash away all the blood shed down the ages, settle those great quarrels once and for all. It was the women who helped me. I was the ideal go-between, neither on the side of the anvil nor of the hammer, the neutral umpire—but it was the women who did the work.

"The Tamong Miri business dates back some fifteen years. It's very confused and begins with the murder of a Dutchman—an administrator, I believe. In reprisal the Dutch burned down Tamong Miri's longhouse and killed three men and one woman, the rest of the band

[48]

having had time to make off into the forest. Well, now! Tamong Miri, the murderer of the administrator—he's known as the Terrible because he's an ugly customer— then pounces in fury on the neighboring village, which had provided the Dutch with guides, and sacks it. The attack, briskly carried out, results in fourteen villagers killed and twenty-three taken prisoner, mostly women, who are later sold as slaves to the Sulu pirates on the east coast. The Dutch Administration makes matters worse by hitting out in all directions to calm everyone down. You see the complications!

"I discovered all this, bit by bit, thanks to the women. That old rogue Tamong Miri—now half blind, having lost an eye in the skirmish, but still as fearsome as ever—laid all the blame on the traitors who had provided the guides. He held his tribe in his fist like a weapon, ready to use it at my expense if I gave a single rifle to his enemies. Several times I came across war arrows stuck in the ground on my path. The survivors of the attack were demanding the price of a human life for every man killed—fourteen—and as many dragon jars as there were women sold as slaves.

"I spent my days running between the two villages, and my nights drinking ayak and wheedling those bloody numbskulls who went on speechifying endlessly and posturing like outraged noblemen. I had a bout of fever, the ayak made me even worse. I kept sweating and vomiting. And all those palavers, without beginning or end!

"It was the women who encouraged me to go on— otherwise I'd have told them all to go to hell. They

[49]

wanted to come to an agreement quickly because a boy from one clan and a girl from the other were due to be married; the girl, of Tamong Miri's line, was pregnant and the marriage had to be concluded according to the rules before the birth of the baby. They engaged in an invisible termite activity and day by day sapped the men's resistance—the structure was still standing, but behind the façade it was all hollow.

"Eventually, one night, Tamong Miri the Terrible, fiercer and haughtier than ever, asked me to intervene. I advised him, since it was a long-standing affair and the responsibilities were not clearly defined, to forget about the women sold as slaves, and I suggested that the heads of the first fourteen Japanese, whom Tamong Miri's people were bound to kill if they joined the militia, should be given to the plaintiffs to appease the spirits and the spirits of the dead. Thus the blood money would be settled.

"To everyone's surprise, the old one-eyed pirate burst into a loud guffaw.

" 'Your eyes say nothing, but your lips speak well, red man. I see a revival of the days of high adventure.'

"A few days later the matter was formally settled, and the first two militia units were set up. Further reconciliations followed, always at the expense of the poor Japanese. I had become a big chief. Before the south-westerly trade winds returned, I had my army. Only three tribes in the west, on the Red Dogs' borders, had refused to join the movement, but I was relying on the brutality of the Japanese reprisals to bring them over to us sooner or later with their tails between their legs.

"I called a council of the headmen of the tribes at which I proposed stopping payment of the rice tax. It was a stormy meeting. Senghir, who had had a bit of a pasting the year before, was not too keen on inciting the Japanese and had a whole cautious clan backing him, but Tamong Miri the Terrible, my friend since the settlement of the feud, dreaming once again of raiding, looting, carousing, and unrestricted hunting—hoping for the return of the days of high adventure—swept aside all objections. I also suggested that the rice due as tax should be stored as army property and reserved for any village that might suffer Japanese reprisals.

"For the first time in ages, in several centuries perhaps, the old quarrels had been settled, and the tribes had taken a collective decision. This was the birth of a nation. It was going to be necessary to put it to the test for fear it would break down again in fruitless squabbles. The long palavers of the council had already revived futile jealousies like half-extinguished fires. We needed proof of God—that's where the Japanese came in. I only hoped that their reactions would not be too brutal and that the shock would not bring my fragile structure tumbling down. I sent Gwai off to the Red Dogs to bribe the people in contact with the Japanese to keep us posted, then we sat back and waited.

"One moon later—one month, if you prefer—the first reports began to filter through. Substantial reinforcements transported by rail from Beaufort to Tenon were advancing up the Tomani bridle path along the River Padas. Then we received further details. The troops consisted of a battalion who were recruiting

[51]

guides for a push toward the east. Gwai had done a good job, half the guides were on our side. The militias which were standing by began to marshal their forces, while those stationed farther west kept watch on the Japanese movements.

"Now I was going to find out. The judgment of God! A bloody reverse meant collapse, my death, or— even worse—being handed over to the Japanese as the price of peace. There would be no decisive victory—we had simply to try to transform this war into a series of separate engagements, avoid a frontal encounter, and nibble away at the battalion day after day.

"I felt happy, as elated as Tamong Miri, whose one eye glinted with ferocity. I had chosen as the site of my first ambush the deep-sunken upper valley of the Tung-kalis river. Since dawn we had heard them blundering along in the mist like a herd of buffalo. Crouching under cover all around me were three hundred warriors, the bravest, the simplest, the merriest of men, shivering with cold and trembling with impatience. The evening before, our guides had escaped in the dark, and in the morning the Japanese, fearful of being betrayed again, massacred almost all the other native guides. They were thus advancing blind, but I had launched my attack too soon, without waiting for them to send out patrols, and for this mistake we paid a heavy price. They remained in close formation, each group providing covering fire for its neighbor. By midday Tamong Miri the Terrible was dead, and fifteen other warriors. We pulled out, leaving a long bloody trail behind us in the jungle.

"That night there was a paralyzing sense of calamity.

Two of the wounded silently died, one after the other. The rest kept whimpering and groaning. I had ordered bonfires to be lit on all the heights overlooking the Japanese in order to mislead them, and they made no attempt to follow us, thank heavens! It was a lovely night and all the stars were out. In the moonlight I could see the expression on the faces of my Comanches, I could tell at a glance that I had lost.

"At dawn there remained no more than fifty around me. One of the wounded who had been screaming all the time finally died. The Japanese resumed their march toward the east and after their departure we found, on the bank of the Tungkalis, the bodies of Tamong Miri and a few other warriors all mixed up with five of theirs. There were also several patches of blood, some blood-stained field dressings, and thirty or so freshly dug graves. The murdered guides had been flung into a communal trench farther off. We recovered a few weapons and a case of grenades that had been left behind.

"So that was that. I had lost.

"By noon Gwai and the original band were the only ones still with me—the rest had gone home after disinterring the dead in order to carry off their heads. But things are never so bad or so good as one thinks at first. Three days later the Japanese air force bombed seven villages, killing several women and children. This acted like a whiplash on my disbanded army.

"The Japanese battalion went stumbling on, lost in the jungle. We resumed our harassing tactics and laid deadly booby traps along their route which further impeded their progress. Guided by aircraft, they eventually emerged by the rapids of the Sembakung and somehow managed to find Senghir's village, which they burned down again before making their way back to Tomani.

"The campaign had lasted two months. We had lost twenty-three warriors. Fifteen women and twelve children had been killed in air raids, and a further twenty seriously wounded. Five villages were totally destroyed. The Japanese must have lost about sixty-five or seventy men, and we had captured over thirty weapons.

"At the council of the tribal headmen which followed, Senghir drank a great deal and cawed loudly like the old crow that he is.

" 'You have maddened us with the smell of blood, and now madness is flooding everywhere, like a torrent in spate digging its bed. You have unleashed the hounds of war and now they will be at our throats until we are all dead. You are not one of us. You are a stranger. Away with you!'

"All eyes were turned on me. I was ill, helpless, tired to death, and Tamong Miri was no longer there to defend the return of the days of high adventure. I said nothing. It was Gwai the Silent, my brother Gwai, who saved me once again.

" 'You say, Senghir, we have come to the point where we will no longer follow him. But the young warriors who followed him from the River Tungkalis to the Sembakung and afterward right up to Tomani, what do they have to say? You say, Senghir, he is not one of us. But was he not found in the Forest of the Spirits? Was his son not born in the Forest of the Spirits? You say, Senghir, he is a stranger. Yes, he is a stranger. A stranger, just as salt is a stranger to rice. But tell me, O Senghir, what is the taste of rice without salt?'

"It's almost impossible for me to describe the days that followed. I was ill, I was exhausted, perhaps I had gone mad again. My emaciated body was once more a mass of boils and ulcers. And while the militias, battered but not beaten, made their way back to their villages with the heads and sometimes the weapons of the enemy, while in front of the ayak jars at night the poets composed a new legend about heroes and the red man with gray eyes, I was afraid I might start howling again in the dark.

"If you had come then . . . Perhaps it was not too late.

"Dying is nothing. Death? Life? Life is within us, it stirs and dreams of stirring forever. When we are dead, life goes on, it is there, still stirring. I have seen a corpse that was alive. An old Japanese corpse that had been lying out on a track in the sun for three whole days. It was alive. Its belly was rising and falling in an irregular rhythm. Its eyes were moving. It was dribbling at the mouth and from time to time it uttered a human groan. As I passed close by—I suppose the vibration of the earth must have shifted its strangely rigid forearm with the clenched fist pointed at the sky—the warm hand gripped my ankle and I felt things moving under the skin of the palm, which was wrinkled like a glove. In the dark it emitted a faint glow, and if one stayed still long enough one could see and hear it wriggling.

"No! I'm not frightened of death any more. I'm not frightened of pain either. I'm . . . I'm frightened of myself.

"I hadn't meant to tell you, but I'm going to all the same. When I left my mates, after the shipwreck, I made for the forest. I didn't want to be a prisoner, I wanted my freedom. Have you ever been in prison? Freedom is merely a word, but I know what it really means. I made for the forest. I didn't want to follow the others. I don't know, it was some power that . . . I can't say what. I didn't want to, that's all. Later on I heard the sound of firing, so I think I was right.

"I kept marching during the day, and at night I used to creep into the isolated huts of the Malays after reconnoitering them closely. I didn't even have to threaten them with my rifle to make them give me something to eat; my eyes were enough.

"And then I got to where the real jungle begins. There were no more Malays, no more houses, only trees. At night, all alone, I was frightened. During the day I kept marching, but every night I was a bit more frightened. I was plunging into horror. One morning I threw away my rifle because I knew I was going to kill myself that night, and the following morning, trembling all over, I retraced my steps and looked for it wildly for hours, foraging in the undergrowth which tore me to shreds, as though my life depended on it. My life!

"I swear I would have killed myself if I had found it. Every rustle in the jungle sent a fresh wave of fear surging through me. I felt oppressed, suffocated by the

[56]

trees, I longed for the sky. I spent three days shivering with hunger and cold on a mountain top above the clouds, but at night the fear was still there. I went deeper and deeper into the forest. When I could no longer walk, I dragged myself along and stopped for hours, dazed, before struggling on again. When darkness fell I feverishly dug myself a hole with my nails and curled up inside it like an animal about to die, but I was alive and at night the fear was still there. I was submerged by waves of anguish.

"At dawn, frozen and almost dead, I used to beseech God with tears in my eyes to spare me the following night. Once I yelled at the sky, which I was unable to see, 'I've done more than my share. Now it's up to You!'

"I don't know how many days or weeks this lasted. My mind was failing, I had no strength left, and every night I was a prey to horrors. It was more terrifying than the depths of the ocean, more terrifying than the void of the sky. I was reduced to sheer terror, every cell in my body was convulsed by terror. Sharp-pincered insects were burrowing into my brain to devour it. Leeches crept into my veins and sucked my blood, into my very heart. Red ants nibbled at my eyes. Flies laid their eggs under my skin, I could feel them hatching out. Worms swarmed everywhere. But all this was nothing. The worst, the unbearable, was my fear, myself.

"I was almost dead but I must still have had enough strength to howl at night, because that's how Gwai found me. He was on his way back from hunting. That's how it was."

[57]

Learoyd fell silent. Some time later he added in a low voice: "What a long, long way!"

Far off the thunder prowled, growling like a wild beast. The stars had disappeared, and every now and then sheet lightning blazed soundlessly, illuminating the nearby jungle, a somber cliff rearing suddenly into a stormy sky whose reddened image persisted on the retina long after the return of darkness. The air was oppressive, still, broken by heavy breathing, sudden sighs, creakings, patterings; the slumbering longhouse, a fragile vessel lost in the vast ocean of darkness, was still stirring with life. I was slightly drunk, and I felt all this warm, comforting life as keenly as the throbbing in my temples.

Abruptly Learoyd stood up, causing confusion among the dogs crouched in the shadows. The boards of the bamboo floor yielded under his weight.

"I talk too much."

His voice had become dry, almost harsh.

"I always talk too much."

He took a few uncertain steps, picked up a torch and turned to me. I was still lying on the floor, my head resting on my rolled-up parachute. He really did look very young, his hair aflame in the orange torchlight, his eyes cold, metallic, devoid of expression.

"I didn't do all this for King and Country—I'm a free man. In this place, I'm King. I wanted to try to tell you how I . . . why I am master here.

"No, I'm not mad! I don't howl at night any more, I was tired, that's all. I'm no longer frightened of the jungle either—I'm a long way past all that. I'll never go back to England, or to Ireland. This is my home. I was born in the Forest of the Spirits, where Gwai found me. My son was born in the Forest of the Spirits, and he'll become King at my death. We don't need you."

Learoyd moved off a few steps and added over his shoulder, "Goodnight, I'll see you tomorrow. I'll have my Comanches escort you up north to the Sulu pirates, who fight for money, or down south to the Dayaks, who fight for the British. You can take your choice!"

Gwai, who had been crouching in the shadows like a dark ghost, silently rose to his feet and vanished in Learoyd's wake.

"I can understand that fellow," Anderson muttered. "He's afraid we might queer his pitch. What a shambles!"

Then he got ready for bed. A little later he added, "It's not bad stuff, that ayak, but it's deceptive," and he snuffed out the last torch.

There were a couple of dogs fighting somewhere in the dark. I flung one of my jump boots at them to quiet them and heard them bolt, with the rest of the pack at their heels.

Today, in my study, in front of this blank sheet of paper on which I am trying to make him live again, it is very difficult for me to believe in the reality of Learoyd's existence. Yet I should not like to betray him a second time, because that would be to betray myself. He was that young man who resembled me like a brother. He was my youth.

Night falls early in England in winter. It's cold. Raining. Not the fearful downpour of the tropics, but a gentle drizzle, as mild and melancholy as old age.

I have drawn the curtains. I can no longer see the lights shimmering on the gray waters of the old river, but I can still hear the hooting of the trains at Mugby Junction and the ceaseless hum of the city like the turbines of a great ocean liner. I am alone in my study with my books. For me it's all over, I've cast anchor. My timbers are encrusted with seaweed and barnacles. I shall voyage no more.

I shall never again see Borneo, its coast dark against the dazzling sea, never again see the northeasterly monsoon sky with its swollen clouds towering to a height of thirty thousand feet. I shall never again feel that warm wind, still moist from having swept over the waves of the South China Sea, bringing a smell of quagmire, leaf mold, rotting wood, and a faint whiff of iodine. I shall never again make my way up the great red rivers, along tracks buried in forests like cathedrals, toward the blue mountains. My quest is over; it all lies behind me, together with the dreams of Learoyd, who believed himself to be a king, a poet, and a captain: blurred shadows in the darkness of this winter which will never know the blossoming of spring. "Man that is born of woman is of few days, and full of trouble. He cometh forth like a flower, and is cut down: he fleeth also as a shadow, and continueth not."

The only thing that will survive from those days of high adventure is this Nepenthes, the pitcher plant which I discovered on August 6, 1945—the day of the bombing of Hiroshima—on the slopes of the Great Mountain of the Dead overlooking the Plain of Elephants in the East, and on which I have bestowed a name.

What's become of Learoyd? Is he still alive? The last time I saw him, after betraying him, a few days before they hanged the Japanese colonel whose name I have forgotten, he was mute and already living as though dead. If he has managed to survive, he has no doubt joined the huge retreating throng of defeated men, sinking listlessly into oblivion. So I, who knew him as a king, might pay him the most glowing tribute: this dazzling, ardent flame of youth, whose rosy light still tinges the horizon behind us like a fabled city that has been pillaged and set on fire.

Yes, Learoyd is a dream and I hope he is dead. Life is a holocaust of dreams, a graveyard of dreams trampled underfoot, betrayed, sold, abandoned, forgotten. What a mess!

Yet he was there that night, almost naked, in the midst of his wretched people, with his strange tattoo, his gray eyes, and his red locks like a banner of revolt. He was there, lit by smoking torches, in that miserable straw hut lost in the depths of a dismal jungle, and he said it was a kingdom. I, fascinated and covetous, wanted to steal it from him. Mad! We were mad!

Next day, I remember, when we climbed to the top of the ridge to install our transmitter, he indicated with a sweeping gesture the whole drenched panorama and declared proudly,

"It's all mine. And if you march ten days and ten nights in any direction, it's still all mine."

There was nothing to see, only wind and rain.

He was no more able to prevent himself from talking than he had been able to prevent himself from feeling terrified in the darkness of the jungle. It was not in Gwai, in Tamong Miri the Terrible, or in that old crow Senghir that he had confided; it was in me, a man of his own race, perhaps his most dangerous opponent. What terrible loneliness lay concealed behind the vacancy of his eyes. He had tried to control himself, to say no more than was necessary, but the pressure had been too great, the steam had escaped in a piercing whistle. A cry? A call for help? Poor devil! (We were, in those days, as cruel and indifferent as young animals devoid of imagination! I killed, or ordered others to kill, with less emotion that I now feel at seeing a tree felled when our woodlands are massacred for the sake of highways.)

During that starless night, I thought only of dethroning him. Once the last torch had been extinguished, and I lay leaning on my parachute, drunk, I dreamed of taking possession in my turn of this fantastic kingdom which sprang to life and vanished as the lightning flashed. Not for a moment did I contemplate making my way to the Dayaks or the Sulu pirates. It was *this* territory that I would stamp with my seal, even if I had first to confront Learoyd the Magnificent in single combat. I had a weighty argument to overcome his determination: Liberators laden with containers of arms and ammunition.

Eventually I fell into a restless sleep, only to wake shortly afterward bathed in sweat. I thought I had heard a howl. A dog perhaps? Or some wild beast? Or even the storm, which had drawn nearer? The stillness of the air was oppressive; lightning flashes, more and more frequent, silently ripped the night apart.

I woke up again a little later, ill at ease. It was pitch dark and I couldn't have seen my hand in front of my eyes. A distant roar, like that of the sea, approached at the speed of a galloping horse, the jungle creaked, a warm scent-laden breath swept the veranda, and the whole longhouse quivered in wild gusts of wind. Then there was nothing but the gritty sound of the rain, as

[63]

though buckets of gravel were being poured on the thatched roof. I went outside for a few seconds. The cold water streamed over me, dispelling the last traces of drunkenness.

I curled up soaking wet in my parachute and fell fast asleep until dawn.

A sinister dawn, devoid of color or shadow. A real hang-over morning, as Anderson said. The sky was gray, the rain was gray, even the jungle was gray. Everything was gray, cold, and dank. The kingdom was showing its true face: a few acres of mud and trees. I had a splitting headache.

It took me over an hour to shake Learoyd's determination. He had arrived in a suspicious, obdurate mood, followed by his shadow, Gwai the Silent; it was only after I had mentioned plane-loads of arms that I felt his interest quicken. I then proposed an alliance with him and pointed out that I was treating him more or less as a foreign potentate and not as a British Army sergeant. He laughed but said nothing in reply.

"Now listen to me," I told him. "There'll soon be general hostilities in Borneo. The Australians are going to land. In the south, other teams like mine are organizing the Dayaks of Sarawak. In the north, the Americans are arming the former Sulu pirates. Join us, you and your people, and if Darwin agrees we'll equip and instruct the Comanche army. Otherwise, I'm afraid you and your savage tribes will be swept aside."

Learoyd conferred at great length with Gwai, who was still as impassive as a sphinx. I guessed from his voice that he was trying to convince his friend—his brother, as he called him. With a glance, I made Anderson understand he was to set up the transmitter and saw him disappear into the pouring rain to sling the aerial between a couple of trees.

I was extremely conscious of the responsibility I was taking in relying on Learoyd; I was reinforcing, almost officially confirming, his power over the Muruts, but I believed everything he had told me the night before, and I had neither the time nor the means to verify whether or not his position was as strong as he claimed. I also thought that everything would fall into place as soon as my instructors took charge of his army. After all, my objective was to rally the tribes to fight against Japan, and I would have made an agreement with the devil himself to attain it.

This was a mistake, and I deserve all the charges against me that subsequently accrued, except that of failing to threaten with a court-martial "that crazy sergeant who thought he was a king." He would have laughed until he cried.

In the end Learoyd accepted my offer, and to seal our alliance I gave him my American carbine, which he had examined with such interest at our first encounter. While I was trying to draft a message for Darwin, Anderson reappeared, boisterous and running with water like a gutter, followed by a horde of naked little bodies.

The shower had put him in a good humor. He shook himself cheerfully in the midst of the children, who kept piping: "Good morning, sir! Good morning, sir!"

I instructed him to keep them quiet and start sending our call signal on the required frequency. The cries ceased and, all together, the little faces with their anxious eyes turned to me. I felt slightly ashamed of having spoiled their fun, but the drafting of the message was quite tricky; it was while struggling over the wording that I suddenly realized the absurdity of the whole situation. How could I explain to officers comfortably ensconced in headquarters some eighteen hundred miles away that I had landed in the heart of a kingdom belonging to an Irish NCO who, having had me trussed up by his subjects and threatened with deportation, deigned nonetheless to accept an alliance with the British Empire to help him wage a personal war against the armies of the Rising Sun? I could just imagine the expression on the face of Colonel Fergusson of Special Forces! In fact I did see it a few months later. He was foaming with rage and consigning to the devil both me and "my crazy sergeant who thought he was a king."

I finally decided to make a full report in a facetious tone, ending with a request for a drop of arms, ammunition, and instructors to organize the Comanche army and for confirmation of my status as Ambassador to His Majesty. I also signaled the position of the enemy posts at Tomani and along the River Padas, which Learoyd had shown me on a map captured from the Japanese.

At this time all maps of the interior of Borneo still showed blank; only general contours and the course of

[67]

main rivers were sketched in, either very approximately or with dotted lines, but Learoyd had filled his in. It was a remarkable achievement; with a bird's quill dipped in homemade ink, he had drawn in the smallest torrents, tracks, passes, and villages, inscribing the Murut name of each feature in the phonetic language he had invented. It looked like a medieval chart.

I discovered the bounds of his kingdom, which extended into the Sultanate of Sarawak and penetrated, in the southeast, deep into the former Dutch colony. He also showed me the spot where Gwai had picked us up, and by checking against my own map I realized that the navigator of the Liberator had been mistaken in the valley. If we had been dropped according to plan, Senghir's Comanches would have received us. I subsequently met this old headman, who really did look like a plucked crow and even had an unpleasant cawing voice. He was jealous of Learoyd's authority, and I always wondered what would have happened if . . .

The downpour persisted. The heavy drops drummed on the thatched roof with exasperating regularity. I struggled with the complicated code I had been given in Darwin: the classical five-letter-group double-transposition cipher requiring two big books. The slightest mistake was liable to render the message completely incomprehensible.

Anderson thought he had picked up Morotai, but so faintly that he snatched off his earphones and growled, "We're in a hollow here, sir. We'll have to move to that crest up there, then I'm bound to get through."

[68]

In the early afternoon we set off, hammered as soon as we stepped outside by the streams of water pouring off the roof, to climb to the crest hidden in the clouds. In a few moments my battle-dress was reduced to a cold rag clinging to my skin. Learoyd and Gwai accompanied us, with the group of Comanches originally detailed to escort us back to the frontier; they now carried the transmitter. I was carrying nothing. I was in good training, yet I found it difficult to keep up with them. The rotting slime of the steep slope afforded no firm foothold for my mud-caked jungle boots. Several times I slipped and rolled in an avalanche of rotting vegetation before managing to latch on to some creepers. Learoyd went barefoot, his toes gripping the ground like claws, and he advanced with the steady gait of the hillmen. He had cut himself a switch of bamboo with which he flicked away the leeches climbing up his bare thighs.

We reached the clouds and the rain stopped, but the air was so laden with moisture that I did not notice. The mist-shrouded forest was steeped in the dank, chilly, glaucous atmosphere of an underwater cave. The trail was covered with reddish moss as thick as a sponge, revealing here and there the blue metallic sheen of some insect with a hard shell that cracked under the Comanches' bare feet. Huge spiders' webs condensed the moisture into strings of gray pearls. The creatures themselves, jet black and as big as a man's fist, with a yellow death's head on the abdomen, darted out from their lairs one after another to confront us as we approached. Gwai slashed one of them in two with his sword and I

[69]

saw the separate halves, still living, wave their long, hairy, crablike legs in an attempt to escape and hide in some hole.

The mountaintop was a rocky platform covered in bushes and Kunai grass. The clouds, which had lifted slightly, drifted heavy and gray above our heads, still shedding a steady flood that rattled, like shrapnel on corrugated iron, on the thick, lusterless grass, six feet high and the thickness of three fingers. Grimy wisps of fog still clung to the ghost of a solitary tree whose dead branches twisted skyward.

I was shivering under the weight of my drenched battle-dress. Learoyd, naked as a Murut except for a sort of loincloth which hung down in front over his thighs, did not appear to feel the cold. His long red matted locks made his head look like a jellyfish. He was laughing.

"This is the Forest of the Spirits. Beautiful, isn't it?" he said, then led me up to a spur overlooking the dark and desolate rift of the valley. The curly black pelt of the jungle stretched blurred and hazy into the distance where it disappeared behind the rampart of rain. It was dismal as death.

"It's all mine."

The Comanches quickly erected a small straw hut concealed under the nearest trees on the edge of the forest, and Anderson installed his transmitter inside it. A fire was lit, I undressed to wring out my clothes and removed a dozen leeches, warm, gorged with blood, thick as my thumb, which had fastened themselves round my waist and in my groin. Anderson flicked his into the flames, enjoying the sight of them squirming and sizzling.

The rain stopped suddenly, and almost at once the crest was bathed in scorching sunshine. As on the previous day, I had the uncanny impression that all the vegetation was sprouting before my eyes with savage violence. Here was original life, oozing, bubbling, fermenting like some huge culture medium. The warm wind wafted the smell of rich silt, sickening whiffs of fecund earth laden now and then with scents of exotic flowers.

The sinister landscape itself was transformed. To the west, the great trees of the Forest of the Spirits extended in a stream of emeralds down to the valley bottom and the torrent, which sparkled in the sun between strips of velvety black shade. The air was very clear, and you could see big monkeys leaping from branch to branch and disappearing in the foliage. To the east, long jagged islands in dragon's-back formation emerged from an ocean of clouds gray as the Atlantic in winter, and far, far on the horizon white-crested waves broke against the flanks of a blue mountain.

I was dazzled by the great beauty of it all.

"That's the Great Mountain of the Dead," Learoyd told me. "Beyond is the Plain of Elephants, and after that the sea."

He contemplated this fleeting beauty, this delicate balance of form and color, with the gravity of a peasant

[71]

whose feet are planted solidly in the earth, and his next words startled me:

"They'll have to leave us a gateway to the sea."

I looked at him, not understanding. "The Japanese?"

"No, the others, the rest of the world. After the war."

I know now that he meant a direct access to the coast and to salt for his people, but at the time his remarks were utterly incomprehensible. I had no time to question him further; Anderson was calling out excitedly, "I've got them, sir! I've got them loud and clear!"

In the straw hut one of the Comanches on the saddle of the portable generator pedaled as if on a treadmill, to provide the necessary current for Anderson, who was feverishly tapping out his call sign. The rhythmic, regularly spaced replies from Darwin crackled through the static in the receiver; the operator at the other end was obviously calm and relaxed.

The identification procedure was lengthy. After dropping us into the unknown, Special Forces HQ had only one worry: our being "compromised," by which euphemism they meant our being captured by the Japanese and interrogated until we revealed the secret of the code. An accident of this sort occurred in Europe—in Holland, I believe. Not only was there a blood bath in the Resistance, but—what was worse in the eyes of the Service—the Germans deceived us for months on end with false intelligence. An absolute disaster! To minimize these risks, Colonel Fergusson had worked out a series of security checks, peculiarities, and deliberate errors on the part of each operator; if these errors did not occur during transmission, it meant that the operator had been "compromised," and any information he sent back was discounted.

At last Anderson turned to me, beaming all over his face, and announced, "We can go ahead, sir. Let's have the message."

There was a faint hum outside, rising slowly above the crackling of the radio. Some Comanches extinguished the fire without making any smoke, using a heap of ash which they had evidently prepared for this purpose, while the rest took cover under the trees and stayed there without moving. Two big twin-engine Betty bombers came roaring over the ridge at ground level.

I gestured to Anderson to stop transmitting; immersed in his work, he had not noticed the noise of the airplane. He looked at me, eyes wide and mouth open, and instinctively lowering my voice, I muttered, "Japanese!"

The war we had both forgotten now burst upon us with a noise of thunder, and it was like a shadow in sunlight. I had a shattering sense of failure, of being guilty of negligence, of not getting on fast enough. There was a war on, and I was playing around with a lunatic! I was overwhelmed by the stupidity of my behavior. The feeling lasted only a moment, but it had the force of those awakenings in the first light of dawn after a night of drinking when one contemplates one's whole life with cruel lucidity.

The two bombers were coming back. The last Comanche in the hut, the one pedaling the generator, was curled up on the ground in the foetal position and lay as though dead. Anderson gaped at me. I was unable to

[73]

move a muscle. I was waiting for the machine-gun burst that would absurdly put an end to this whole business.

Apparently the Comanches had made a good job of camouflaging the straw hut. The two airplanes circled without spotting us. With their flaps down, they glided over so low and so slowly that from time to time I glimpsed the leather-helmeted pilots leaning over to peer down; one of them had slipped his goggles up on his forehead.

The plexiglass cockpits glinted for the last time in the sun, the flaps retracted into the wings, and the heavy machines roared off again, dipping into the valley like a couple of sharks diving in deep water. For some time we heard them roaming around far below us before they flew off to the west and the Sembakung.

"Those bastards have got a ruddy nerve," Anderson growled. "With a decent rifle I could have put a bullet between their eyes."

A little later a dull rumble, like distant thunder, rolled from crest to crest toward us. Learoyd looked at Gwai, who gave the ghost of a smile.

"It's Senghir catching it again," he explained to me cheerfully. "He's got no luck, they're always clobbering him."

Meanwhile the weather conditions had deteriorated somewhere in the Celebes Sea between Borneo and the Halmaheras, and Anderson had some difficulty in re-establishing contact with Morotai; the signals were faint and distorted with atmospherics. He finally succeeded, after several attempts, in transmitting the whole of my message, and I left him to spend the night in the hut—

with the mosquitoes, flies, hornets, leeches, and a few Comanches—to receive the reply from Darwin. I cast a last glance at the Mountain of the Dead, whose blue slopes had turned deep purple in the rays of the setting sun; then we climbed down to the valley.

As we reached the longhouse in the muggy darkness flickering with stars and fireflies, the Comanches burst into a strange song. It did not have the melancholy rhythm of the Murut dirges; it evoked different feelings from the oppressive atmosphere of the jungle; it sounded almost familiar to me. All of a sudden I recognized it. It was *The Wearing of the Green:*

For they're hanging men and women too . . .

Learoyd had adopted it as his military anthem, and the naked warriors were simply mouthing the words without understanding what they meant.

That night we again drank ayak sitting under the veranda in the acrid pipe smoke. Behind us, on the bamboo partitions, our shadows danced to the rhythm of the torch flames. Yoo was there. This was the first time I met her. She had the broad, slightly flattened face peculiar to all the inhabitants of the interior, a well-turned nose though somewhat fleshy at the base, lips rather too thick and sensual. But what I remember best is the freedom and confidence of her movements, the insolent beauty of her firm, stocky body and, above all, the dramatic intensity of her jet-black eyes. Distress, like the eyes of my dog when I gave him to a friend on leaving for the war (I have never had another dog!). I had the feeling that I frightened her. To her I was an indefinable danger, an unknown menace.

I still wonder today what sort of picture she could have had of the world from which I came. Nothing very pleasant surely, something horrible enough for the man she loved to have braved the hell of the jungle to escape from it.

Learoyd had taught her a few words of English, which she pronounced with rolling r's. She greeted me with a hesitant smile which revealed her small white even teeth, "Good morning."

Learoyd burst out laughing. "I like that. You ought to say: 'Good night.' " He turned to me, "I've never been able to make her understand."

She solemnly repeated, "Good night," but there was no smile now. Learoyd, who was watching her, spoke to her in Murut, and the smile slowly reappeared on her lips.

"She was cross, so I reminded her how they all used to laugh at me at first when I tried to speak their language. Surely I'm entitled to get my own back a bit. It's true! I used to spend night after night walking along the torrent, bawling out words that were impossible to pronounce. I even tried with pebbles in my mouth. Listen to this . . ."

Twice he enunciated a word that sounded like "biiri."

"You didn't notice the difference, did you? Well, the first time it meant the great dragon of the depths who overturned the earth to make the mountains in the legend of the creation of the world. The second time it meant a mat, that's all, just a mat. A sleeping mat. You do it with your throat. The first time you breathe out, the second time you breathe in. Watch my Adam's apple. It took me at least three months to get the hang of it."

He re-embarked on his demonstration and, sure enough, his Adam's apple quivered when he repeated the word, but I still failed to notice any difference in the pronunciation.*

Night slid gently on. Yoo's dark gaze kept slipping away from mine, only to return and rest upon me with the same silent apprehension every time I looked away. Poor girl! Perhaps some imperceptible sign already gave her a presentiment of evil, just as horses snort and shy long before the occurrence of a cataclysm. Outside, in the moonlight, the jungle seemed to be waiting.

I had drunk hardly anything, just enough to make me feel in form. The scruples I had felt that afternoon when the airplane came over no longer disturbed me. That was the last time I had any doubts about the successful outcome of my mission. Later on I had neither the time nor the inclination to doubt: I was too busy living. The Japanese were far away and the rest of the world farther still; I had sent off my first message; everything was in order.

* One of my colleagues, Professor Sherwood, a distinguished linguist and phonetician, has since explained to me that this was probably a question of preglottalized consonants: a phenomenon which is found in Tahitian, among the Nagas of Assam, the Mois of Indochina and, in general, among all the natives of the Indian Archipelago.

[77]

I would certainly have felt less serene if I had known that at that very moment Dick Fergusson was wondering if I was "compromised" or if I had had a "hard landing" —another of the Colonel's euphemisms. Once, on a training jump, an Australian sergeant had got his feet entangled in the rigging lines of his parachute and had landed on his head. He had been out of his mind for several weeks and was still not completely recovered when I took off for Borneo. He suffered from occasional attacks during which he was unable to bear the sight of any rank senior to his own!

Fergusson, extraordinarily suspicious, at first believed that the facetious tone of my message and my improbable reference to an Irish king were intended to convey a warning that I was no longer free. Going carefully through the text, however, he eventually came across all the sacrosanct security checks, and being reassured on that score, he then settled for a "hard landing." Apparently he even wanted to cable to Morotai to have the crew of the Liberator interrogated and find out how the drop had gone: in vain, as it turned out, since the airplane had been shot down the night before over the Philippines.*

---

* Poor navigator, whom I had cursed when he was already dead! No trace was ever found of the airplane and its American crew. After the war, when it was possible to consult the Japanese archives, no reference to it was ever discovered, but the unexplained disappearance of a Zero in the area patrolled by the Liberator on that day leads me to think that the two aircraft may have fought a duel to the death over some deserted spot. Our pilot, a tall, fair, easy-going boy from Cleveland, Ohio, had said to me before embarking, "I must get me a Zero one day, the Japs can't be as good as they say."

[78]

The next morning, though cold and gray again, was a glorious day. Anderson came rushing down from his cloud-veiled crest in a state of great excitement and waved the reply from Darwin under my nose. No message ever gave us so much delight.

The ensuing weeks were the most exciting of the war for me. The most exciting of my life. If I stop and look back, I feel as though I am sinking beneath a series of billowing green waves. The memories unfurl and I am lost in them . . . lost.

Flares in the dark and the rumbling of Liberators laden with arms, raucous voices and hoarse cries, long marches and still longer intervals of inactivity, sun and salt wind, faces, especially faces: Gwai the Sphinx, Senghir, Anderson, and all the others—anonymous faces which appear clearly for a moment before vanishing again in the darkness of oblivion, as though the beam of a searchlight had swept across them. And others still, the dead: Tamong Miri the Terrible, whom I never knew but who was the legend of the days of high adventure; the Japanese colonel, the warlord hanged at dawn like an outlaw; Fergusson, a character straight out of Kipling. All those destinies disrupted by the bursting of a grenade, those disordered dreams cut short by the thud of a bullet. All those lives chaotically intermingled, occasionally interrupted, and seeming to make no sense.

"A tale told by an idiot, full of sound and fury, signifying nothing!"

In the context of the world war the Learoyd incident was of no more importance than the massacre of the dogs around Tomani and along the River Padas which we had decreed in case their barking should betray our nocturnal activities to the Japanese, of no more importance than that great oak felled outside my father's vicarage in Wales to enable the road to be widened. And yet . . .

My father was a parson. I remember him as a tall, heavy, stern, majestic man. At the age of eighteen I had my first adventure with a woman. I don't know how he came to know about it, he never mentioned it to me, but on the following Sunday the subject of his sermon was sinful woman:

"Such is the way of sinful woman; she eateth, and wipeth her mouth, and saith, I have done no wickedness. Man is like that woman; he may say, I have done no wickedness, but he knows he is lying."

Mere words, I thought. Yet that very evening my father, that austere man who seemed to have no doubts about himself, who seemed to have an absolute faith in the order of the universe, locked himself up in the quiet retreat of his book-lined study and started drinking. When he died, three years later, he had become a drunkard. What beast, what devil lurking in the depths of his soul, was he trying to exterminate or flee?

Biologists think flight is something so basic that it is found in even the most primitive forms of animal life,

[81]

that this may even be one of the fundamental differences between vegetable and animal life. In essence, does man himself represent a form of escape? Anderson told me one night that during the German bombardments of Tobruk he used to cower in his hole, shut his eyes, and try desperately to think of the bodies of naked women: the only image powerful enough to dispel his fear. Naked women!

And what about Fergusson, Colonel Fergusson, DSO, MC, etc., self-assured and triumphant, who, on his way back to England in October 1946 on a P & O liner, threw himself into the sea somewhere between Colombo and Aden? You never know what goes on inside a man.

Tonight, here in my study, hemmed in by solitude, cold, drizzling rain, and the rumble of the city punctuated by the hooting of railway engines, I, like my father, like Fergusson, like Anderson, am in flight; not via lascivious naked women, or neat gin, or the final ocean, but via Learoyd the Magnificent, in a kingdom so distant and so inaccessible that for most of mankind it does not exist.

If I draw up the balance sheet of my life, what is there left? Three slim volumes which a touch of vanity prompted me to bind in leather and keep on a special shelf in my study: *Equatorial Flora,* published in 1936, revised and corrected in 1947, *Orchids of Asia,* and *Stones and Flowers of Wales.* That's all. I was born, I have written three books, I shall die. This is the reality. Dust to dust. And yet what is this paltry reality weighed against the tumultuous dreams of my youth, against the incommunicable emotions which plucked at my heart-strings, against beauty, horror, joy, darkness, and anguish?

Does Anderson in his solitude still dream of naked women? With the passing of the years he must have lost some of his innocence and introduced a few perversions into his dreams. Did my father exterminate the devil? And did Colonel Fergusson, that rock of certainty, try in spite of everything to swim a few strokes, hesitating for the first time in his life on the threshold of the last doorway? Or did he sink like a bar of lead into the infinite depths of the sea from the surface he wished to flee forever?

Of all of us, Anderson chose the commonest form of flight, the first doorway. One of my former pupils, now a playwright, used to say that nothing could hold a candle to a naked woman, neither the finest poetic passage nor the most closely knit dramatic plot, neither laughter nor tragedy. Never, he told me, had one of his plays attained the sovereign power of a Soho strip joint. Nothing equals the strange fascination of the exciting, desirable, yet disturbing female sex. The young Murut girls themselves are aware of this and look upon the Mount of Venus as the height of feminine beauty. A beautiful Mount of Venus must be full and firm and fleshy. Yoo's, if one is to believe the bawdy talk of the kingdom, was the loveliest of all; it had been fashioned by the Spirits.

The Muruts have facile tongues; with the help of ayak in the evenings, the young girls chatting with the boys feel no embarrassment at extolling the gleaming luster of their thighs or the velvet texture of their bellies.

[83]

Some mornings, in the pale mist and soft light of dawn, I used to see Yoo and her companions climb out of the torrent, erect and naked, protecting their private parts with their left hand like a man. They would choose a flat pebble on the bank and, standing with one foot on a rock, would unconcernedly polish their knees and legs. The first time Learoyd looked at me and laughed, and stupidly I blushed. He was extremely proud of his wife's beauty and had composed in the traditional manner some erotic little verses to her glory, which delighted the wise men of the council and made even Gwai smile:

Yoo has the nocturnal gait of a leopard,
Yoo has a gleaming skin, clawed and nibbled with love,
Yoo has pubic hair as silken as a wild boar's withers,
Yoo is more beautiful than the whole Comanche army
    drawn up in order of battle,
Yoo's sex is Yoo's and Yoo has given it to me.

Or:

I do not eat my rice until Yoo has cooked it for me to
    perfection.
I do not penetrate Yoo until her sex is as moist as a frog.

Or again:

The blade of the sword should slip as neatly into the scabbard
As I slip into Yoo when our bodies conjoin in love.

The translation gives only a dull reflection of the rhythm, the resonant richness of these daring cascades of alien words which sing out like pure poetry.

Learoyd loved Yoo, but this did not prevent him from being the lover of several pretty girls from the

[84]

other villages in his territory. One day, when I mentioned this to him, he replied, "If a king can't sleep with a girl who takes his fancy, what's the point of being a king?"

Yoo loved Learoyd. When he stayed away overlong to settle the Tamong Miri business, she heard that he was not spending every night at the council. In a fury she went off and moved into Senghir's longhouse, where she lived with one of her cousins. Learoyd was promptly informed of this, whereupon he returned, picked up his sword, and brought his wife home, as a man should. During the two days' journey he marched ahead of her while she kept thirty paces behind him, and not once did he turn around.

Learoyd and Yoo loved each other. Not that romanticized passion, those strayings of a wayward heart that novels chronicle. Something much simpler: they were a perfect pair. There existed between them that close companionship found in a man and woman who have already come a long way together, a companionship apparent in everyday matters, in looks exchanged, even in silences. Learoyd had taken Yoo into his confidence; she shared his dream and did not fail to provide him with valuable information on the affairs of the kingdom.

The world grows older; each generation dismisses more callously the humanity of its youth, but both Learoyd and Yoo, by some freak of fate, had retained a touch of that mythical original innocence. Not because they were living in a primitive society—primitives are as far

[85]

removed from innocence as we are; they wear blinkers, they are fettered by taboos, prohibitions, traditions lost in the night of time—but because it was their nature. They were two magnificent animals. They ate, drank, made love, traveled the forest trails, and killed with the simplicity of God. They were the glorification of that flesh which we are always seeking to nail to the cross. They were free, greedy, uncouth, ignorant. But they also knew anxiety: they sensed heavy weather approaching over the horizon, and it was not the huge clouds of the northeasterly monsoon.

It was Senghir, the scrawny old crow with the frog-like belly, who gave me the best definition of Learoyd. Crouching in the ruins of his longhouse, he smiled to show his teeth, because his gold-filled jaw was a source of great pride. A long time ago he had served in the Brunei army, and we spoke to each other in Malay.

"A dark sky," he croaked, "never clears without a storm . . ."

He made a gesture of helplessness. His cold eyes were watching me as though I were a prey, or perhaps a last chance.

"We can't do anything about it, he is one of God's afflicted," he concluded.

That was the long and short of it: Learoyd was afflicted of God. A glory and a curse. The time would soon come when I would see him consumed with a thirst for blood which is also a thirst for God. His pride would burst forth in his battle cry: "Learoyd am I!" which linked him to the Middle Ages of the troubadours, dead kingdoms, the Gaelic heroes of Ireland:

[86]

The men whom God made mad
For all their wars are merry
And all their songs are sad . . .

"Learoyd am I!" And the other cry, far more terrible, the cry of the victorious warrior carrying back the head of his enemy. The cry that begins in laughter and ends as a sob.

Sound and fury . . .

Nothing.

I shall stop here for this evening. I'm going to have a stiff whiskey and smoke a Manila cigar. I'll go on again tomorrow at dawn. Learoyd's story is a simple one; it must be told in the quiet manner of a naturalist describing the habits of a rare specimen. I need the stiff chill of dawn. I need its dull gray light which annihilates dreams and phantoms. Tonight I am wandering off the point. The rapture of the night is to be distrusted; it was on a night like this that my father tried for the first time to exterminate the devil. It was on a night like this that Fergusson . . . Or was it at dawn, like the Japanese colonel?

It was cold and gray, it was raining, but that morning the future seemed to stretch before me like a green valley bathed in glorious sunshine, and during the weeks that followed I was as carefree as though I might die the next day or live forever. The reply from Darwin exceeded my fondest hopes. Arms, ammunition, and instructors were pouring in. I was free to organize the Murut kingdom as I saw fit. Fergusson confirmed me in my status of proconsul for a territory as large as Wales. He ended somewhat drily, however, by pointing out that he did not appreciate facetiousness in official reports, and that as far as my mad Irishman was concerned I could make use of him if necessary but must arrange for his evacuation at the earliest opportunity.

Learoyd asked if he could see the message, and with some reluctance I handed it to him; I could hardly do otherwise. He read it through as if he were laughing silently to himself. Then suddenly, almost without transition, his face hardened and his terrible gray eyes bored into me.

"You'd better not try," he murmured softly.

While waiting for my first drop, I had nothing better to do than ponder my action and sort out my dreams. I had landed by sheer chance in a medieval kingdom, but from now on I wanted to know where I was going. How? And why?

The island of Borneo looks like a great crouching beast. In the north, facing the Philippines, is the head, the State of Sabah, owned by the Chartered Company. The neck, opposite Labuan, consists of the tiny independent Sultanate of Brunei. The spine is the Sultanate of Sarawak, the domain of the Rajahs Brook. Finally the belly, in the south, is the huge Dutch colony.

But these divisions are political and artificial. In actual fact there are two Borneos: the coastal zone, which is Malayan and Chinese, rich Moslem and Christian, commercial, open to the foreigner; and the interior, a huge desert of jungle, a mosaic of savage head-hunting tribes, little known, difficult of access, closed in upon itself. The Japanese had occupied the coastal zone but knew virtually nothing about the interior. Only a handful of their units had struggled across it, in 1942, when the island was overrun. Since then they had done no more than carry out a few raids in reprisal against the tribes who refused to pay the rice tax.

Indifferent to political frontiers, Learoyd had built himself a little kingdom, and I had decided to rely on him. His aims were not the same as ours, but he would save us a lot of fumbling and mistakes. After the war, if he did not fall of his own accord, he would have to be eliminated. The Colonial Office and the Dutch would see to that.

[89]

My mission was twofold: to prepare and facilitate future Allied landings and to deny the refuge of the interior to the Japanese. My action would take place simultaneously on two fronts: in the west, where the Japanese were in control of the coast from the oilfields of the Bay of Brunei to the port of Jesselton, including the island of Labuan, and where they had even thrust slightly into the interior along the railway from Beaufort to Tenom, their farthest advance posts running along the River Padas up to Tomani in the country of the Red Dogs; and in the east, where substantial garrisons guarded the harbors of Sandakan (too far to the north for us) and Tarakan.

Our operations would have the characteristics of submarine warfare. Our troops of savages would dive below the vegetation of the vast ocean of jungle; invisible to aerial reconnaissance, they would creep up on the Japanese positions, observe their movements, launch a surprise torpedo attack against their lines of communication, ammunition dumps, and isolated units, then vanish again in deep forest before the enemy reaction had time to make itself felt. If a Japanese armada ventured out on our ocean, it would be broken up, destroyed piecemeal as the big North Atlantic convoys were by German U-boat packs, and disappear from the face of the earth.

I was adopting Learoyd's scheme because it was a good one. There was no question of holding a line of fire or even of giving battle, in the proper sense of the term. We wouldn't be waging war, we would be hunting. A safari. And our quarry would be the most dangerous of all: man.

I made myself drunk on words. I told myself stories like a man in the condemned cell. I re-created the world in my image, like a prophet in the desert. As I said before, I was a young dog. A touching, incurably romantic young dog. I had not been destroyed at birth, and life was only just beginning to train me. I still believed that a thrashing was a game.

The Comanche army would form the nucleus of my troops. I would attach two or three instructors to each militia; they would organize the training of the warriors, recruit others, and lead all of them into battle. I wanted first-rate NCOs so that their personal authority might gradually replace Learoyd's power.

Here I made a mistake in my calculations. Guerrilla warfare develops a taste for individual responsibility, independence, and freedom which sometimes borders on insubordination. The best of my Australians, trained in the spirit of Special Forces, were looking for precisely this sort of unusual life. They, too, were romantic in their own way and the old outlaw blood which always slumbers in the veins of civilized men bestirred itself; they wanted to be gang leaders and lined up quite naturally under Learoyd's banner.

They were meant to take over a kingdom and ended up as the king's bodyguard.

The first drop was to take place three days later. Caution decided me to try it soon after nightfall, when the sky is still clear, so as to avoid an encounter with Japanese fighters. The Liberators would take their bearings from the huge bulk of Mount Kinabalu, follow the Sembakung shimmering in the moonlight as far as a signal fire lit on a mountaintop, then veer to the east along our valley up to the drop zone. This was marked out with fires in the shape of an L, the longer stroke indicating the axis of the drop, with two other fires on the edge of the forest, three hundred yards farther off, marking the end of the zone.

A mass of people had already streamed out of the forest, like ants on the body of an insect, to see the two white men who had fallen from the skies. I knew they were all aware of exactly how Learoyd had greeted Anderson and myself. I was pleased to take my revenge, to display my power a bit and overawe all these wretched savages by showing them

> . . . the shining traffic of Jacob's ladder
> Pitched betwixt Heaven and Charing Cross.

Around the fires, in the dark, there were over a thousand men, women, and noisy children patiently waiting for the show to begin. Anderson summed up my thoughts in his usual laconic style: "This is going to knock 'em in the aisles!"

But the promised miracle did not take place. Morotai had canceled the drop at the last minute, and poor radio conditions prevented them from warning us in time.

Next day, in front of the same crowd, the airplanes turned up dead on time. Visibility was excellent. The two Liberators, like black crosses in the milky light of the stars, flashed on their landing lights as a recognition signal and on the first run dropped four men each. Corbett, an Australian sergeant, had vowed to empty the magazine of his Sten gun as he drifted down, and he treated us to a magnificent firework display with three bursts of tracer bullets, each of which was greeted with cries of delight by the crowd. It might have been a Farnborough air show. My worthy savages were not so very different from an English Sunday crowd; nothing surprised them. Familiarity with the supernatural is one of the characteristics of their life; with them every daily activity has something extraordinary about it: the most commonplace gesture, such as filling a pipe, planting rice, or drinking ayak, is the repetition of a sacred gesture taught by the Spirits. So what was one more prodigy? They had been promised an arrival from the sky, they had seen it, they were content.

Only Learoyd's son, the golden-skinned little fellow with the pot-belly and the gray eyes, was genuinely enthralled. He scampered about among my tall Australians and asked his father for permission to touch them. He really had seen something: there had been thunder, there had been lightning, and the gentle giants had floated down to earth.

The planes reappeared after a wide turn and dropped a score of containers on their second run. I was extremely pleased. Perhaps I had not succeeded in overawing the Muruts, but now I had some men and some weapons; the party could begin.

That night there was a great feast and my Austral-

[93]

ians, in a daze, gulped the ayak as though it was beer. Morotai, I learned, had postponed their arrival by twenty-four hours because our transmitter was working so badly that for a moment they had thought I had had to bolt under threat of Japanese attack. Finally they had taken off from an American base in a bright red sunset, flown through storm clouds lowering motionless over the sea, launched themselves, dry in the mouth, into the dark void, ready to engage in combat forthwith, only to land in the midst of a boisterous peasant carousal from another day and age. It was enough to shake anyone, even close-mouthed Australians, veterans of Tobruk and Cyrenaica.

There were joints of buffalo roasting on the glowing embers, and hordes of yellow dogs prowled around the edge of the firelight, now and then trying to snatch a piece of meat from the men and making off growling under their blows.

From the top of the veranda Learoyd addressed his people, then came and sprawled among us on the parachutes. I asked him what he had said.

"I told them: 'Today our white uncles have come down from the sky with fearsome weapons to help us defend the three forests. The ancients say there are two things that cannot be known, the track of the snake on a rock and the thought in the heart of a stranger. But today I say to you I know their thought. These men come as friends, not masters. They will fight on our side, they will depart when the last Japanese is dead. You must believe me, because I am the one who knows yesterday, today, and tomorrow.

[94]

" 'Drink your ayak and eat your buffalo, for tomorrow we shall fight.

" 'Amuse yourselves, make merry, but do not insult one another, for tomorrow we shall fight.

" 'If you sleep with a woman, there is no problem, for tomorrow we shall fight.

" 'O people of freedom, I have spoken to you straight. Do not forget my words. May the great wind bear them down to the sea and may our enemies tremble.' "

I watched him as he talked, reclining on our parachutes, his elbow on my bag of gold. Yes, it's true, I forgot to mention it—the height of romance—I had a bag of gold! A thousand gold sovereigns. Gold—the good old cavalry of Saint George which wins all the wars by buying up black souls. But the twin souls of the Muruts were not for sale. Most of them had no idea what money was—they practiced barter—and my bag of gold had remained lying there, open but unused.

I listened to Learoyd. He was not content merely to translate his speech; he also tried in his halting English to render the richness of the original. Whom was he deceiving? I pictured him all alone, isolated in this repellent Murut promiscuity—right beside us an idiot woman looked on while mechanically wiping the snot off her child's flattened face with the palm of her hand. Who was he? An imposter, a renegade, or a castaway, a piece of human flotsam? To what was he responding? To some deep-seated prompting of blood, of race, our own race? To some inner voice? To nothing, perhaps?

"You're a good talker," I told him. "That was a fine speech."

"Yes, I have to be," he agreed gravely, and he added with a touch of vanity, "In the whole of my territory there's only Senghir and Gwai, when he feels like it, who talk as well as I do. Before, there was Tamong Miri as well."

"Do you really believe everything you tell them?"

He looked at me for some time without replying.

"You people merely want to win the war," he said at last, "whereas I . . ." He paused, chuckled, and gestured toward the smoked pork and rice. "Eat! When there's food you must eat more than your fill. To satisfy the hunger of yesterday and that of tomorrow. That's another saying—you can say everything with their old maxims."

He himself was neither eating nor drinking. He was sprawled on the pile of parachutes, his head on my bag of gold, naked, destitute, and so youthful, under the idiot stare of a pitiful representative of his free people who was chewing betel with imbecile gravity while nursing a hideous yellow brat.

The thick air reeked of animality, charred meat, and acrid tobacco, mingled with strong human smells. I imagine that the 'tween-decks of the old slave ships must have stunk like this. The sweat streamed down the flushed faces of the tall, close-cropped Australians. There they were: Armstrong, Corbett, Lewis—who was always known as Bren because he was the machine-gun expert —Conklin, and the others whose names I have forgotten, all of them interchangeable in my memory. The only face I remember clearly is Eastward's—a grotesque death mask, round, the size of a pumpkin, with bulging eyes staring at the sun. Eastward had received an explosive bullet in the base of the skull and his head had swelled up like a toy balloon.

Oh, I know their sort pretty well. They were fine soldiers from a fine army, tough, disciplined and efficient, whom a touch of glory, an escapist urge, had launched into adventure. They were the world-weary descendants of those white men who sailed the Seven Seas for spices, gold, for nothing, merely to see if the earth was round. They blasphemed, but they feared God, and their conception of good and evil might have been worse. They were not eloquent, but they knew how to die in silence. They were Anglo-Saxons; they had the pride of their race; they regarded the rest of the world with affectionate disdain.

Learoyd was right: these men would fight, then depart without a backward glance. For the moment they were drinking and guffawing noisily, these worthy comrades-in-arms of mine whose faces I have forgotten.

The Comanches chanted *The Wearing of the Green,* and we had much difficulty in agreeing on what to sing in reply.

Later on there was a great gust of wind which made the torch flames gutter and distorted our shadows, but the rain held off. The woman had not moved; squatting on her haunches, chewing her betel, spitting all over the place, wiping the dirty face of her little monkey, she was still watching us idiotically, as though we were impenetrable enigmas.

"I wonder what goes on in her head," I said out loud.

[97]

Anderson turned around:

"That's Six-Finger Ngee. She's married to Truu, the little Comanche who's got eczema and a protruding navel. She's got two thumbs on her left hand. I don't think she's all there."

I could not get over it. Anderson had spent almost the whole time with his head in the clouds up there on his crest because of our confounded radio communications, yet he knew the inhabitants of the village better than I did. I had already noticed that he had a way with people and was fond of children. Each time he descended from his gloomy perch, at whatever time of day, he was greeted by a chorus of cheerful good mornings.

"Can you manage to tell one from another?" I asked him. "To me they all look alike."

"I'm a sheep breeder, so I know what to look for," he replied.

Then he explained, "When you come across a flock of sheep in a field, they all look alike to you. But not to me. I can distinguish them. I know this one is greedy, that one a scrapper. I distinguish them, you see. They have names. It's the same with these fellows here."

I had never known Anderson to talk so much. Usually he stuck to simple truths and brief observations. I think, now, that he was in perfect harmony with this country. Perhaps even, of all of us, he was the closest to Learoyd. He paid for it, too. At the end of the war Fergusson reduced him to the ranks to teach him discipline and sent him back to his sheep in Queensland.

In the morning there were still a few fires smoking in the mist-shrouded valley. Eighteen containers were lined up like corpses between the piles of the longhouse. The two missing ones were still hanging by their parachutes from the highest branches on the edge of the forest. We had to fell the trees to recover them before the sky cleared in case the Japanese planes might spot the white patches. Conklin, the explosives expert, did the job with a couple of charges.

Learoyd was ill. He lay prostrate on a mat in the section of the longhouse which he occupied with Yoo. He had vomited during the night and Gwai had sent for me. I had taken Corbett along—he was our medical orderly—and he whispered to me at once, "He's dying."

"What's wrong with him?"

Corbett shrugged. "Exhaustion. Dysentery. Malaria as well."

It was a grim specter of Learoyd that I saw lying motionless on the mat, the gray mask of death itself, with its stench and its inevitable concomitant: the abominable buzzing of flies.

Almost always there comes a moment when the need for rest, the need for peace, overwhelms a dying man's will to live; he is too weary, he gives up, he stops, as a shipwrecked man in the immensity of the ocean suddenly ceases to swim. Small outward signs—a flabbiness, a hint of lassitude—appear on the features of the combatant worn out by the long struggle; it is over, he aquiesces, he's already dead. But Death decrees the rendezvous and bides its time. It is less common—except with women—to see the losing battle fought out to the bitter end without reason or hope, and Death obliged to wrest its victory by force. With Learoyd there was no sign, nothing, neither anguish nor doubt nor willingness nor lassitude—nothing. All his energy was concentrated inwardly, and I saw only a scrawny carcass.

When he got up again, a week later, it made me think of those little wedges of wood which can split a rock, of that invisible power which had prompted me to choose botany as a career.

I began to organize my little war. Bren (Lewis) was put in charge of the arms and ammunition and immediately embarked on the instruction of the local militia. The Comanches had never before had many rounds to waste, and their enthusiasm was unbounded. Within two days the best marksmen were grouping their shots in a target the size of a man's head at a range of three hundred yards—Learoyd had already paved the way. I hoped to issue everyone with firearms in a relatively short time, but we decided nevertheless to retain in each militia a flying squad equipped with blowpipes and grenades. This was an abominable stroke of genius: a stroke of genius because the silent efficacy of a blowpipe in a jungle ambush surpassed our hopes, abominable because the death to which the wound from a poisoned arrow condemns a man is more ghastly than one can imagine.

Anderson received reinforcements: a second radio operator. He had already succeeded in turning three Comanches into a source of energy for the generator, and I left him to run his own show. He also occupied himself, of his own accord, with Learoyd's school. He became the English teacher. I was surprised, on returning from a reconnaissance west of the Sembakung, to be greeted by repeated cries of "Good morning, you blokes!"

I dispatched Gwai, Conklin, and a small group to the east, beyond Tamong Miri's village, to reconnoiter the approaches to Tarakan and organize our intelligence network in that area.

By now the Muruts from the surrounding neighborhood were pouring in every day to see me. I transferred my command post to a small straw hut halfway between the longhouse and our radio station, so as to be more independent of Learoyd. I engaged an interpreter, Dali, a great big fellow from up north near the borders of the Red Dogs, who had learned Malayan before the war when working on a rubber plantation. I also distributed my gold—a sovereign as a seal of alliance to every individual I judged to be a man of consequence. Since my criterion was based on the dubious principle that people have the features they deserve, I found myself bestowing the gold

[101]

of the Bank of England on the least ugly faces in the kingdom.

Lieutenant Armstrong was appointed quartermaster, acting officer-in-charge during my absence, and with my mind at peace I prepared to leave for the west. Learoyd suggested coming with me. He had recovered astonishingly quickly. Corbett, without raising any false hopes, had given him all the necessary injections, and Yoo had dosed him with some mysterious brews made from herbs. On the eighth day he got up, pale and emaciated, went for a bath in the torrent, then fell ravenously on a dish of pork and rice. I was reluctant nonetheless to drag him off on a long journey.

"You're too weak," I told him. "You're liable to have a relapse which would kill you."

"Death is lying down and waiting, sleeping. Life is when you get up and march," he replied. "I'm coming with you."

It was an enchanting trip. We set off with a merry escort in the morning, just after the rain, and followed the torrent for six hours as far as the Sembakung. The valley, broad at first, gradually closed in until it was a long, dark gorge, cold and dank, a chasm overhung with disturbing vegetation leaning into the void. At the last bend the air suddenly felt drier, a warm breeze caressed our faces, the roar of the torrent faded, the pale late-afternoon sun dazzled us, and all at once I had the physical impression of freedom. In front of us the great red river rolled silently.

Learoyd, who had brought along the carbine I had given him, amused himself by firing a few shots at some makeshift targets, and the echo of the explosives, so cruelly out of keeping with the serenity of the vast luminous valley, reverberated a long time. The semi-automatic mechanism and the lightness of the weapon fascinated him, but he questioned Corbett at great length as to whether the bullet had sufficient power to stop an advancing man. At sundown he shot a mouse-deer, and we ate it that evening at our halting place.

The mouse-deer is a stupid little animal, appealing but so stupid that it flings itself in panic into the arms of the man stalking it. It is also, under the name of *plandok* or Uncle Bôo, the Fra Diavolo of Murut folklore, the cynical and facetious little sprite of fairytales, who exploits human folly and ridicules human weaknesses. After we had eaten it, roasted with herbs and stuffed with marjoram and green coriander, Learoyd told us one of Uncle Bôo's diabolical adventures.

"Once upon a time there was a man called Boong and a woman called Yoong. They were both very unhappy because they had just buried their child, who had died of hunger. It was during the great drought, when the waters of the Sembakung were reduced to a narrow sky-blue trickle and the foliage of the big trees in the forest turned red. It was when all the buffaloes plunged into the swamp, which is known today as the Graveyard of Horns, and were buried alive in the mud which solidified around them. It was when the spirits themselves took refuge with the dragon Biiri in the bowels of the earth because it was so hot outside, and abandoned the human race, which was left defenseless and without law.

[103]

"Boong had killed a skinny little rat for his son, but when he came back from hunting, his son was dead. Yoong lit a fire to cook the skinny little rat. They both ate it and drank a lot of ayak because they were really very unhappy.

"Uncle Bôo, the mouse-deer, who was famished, smelled the roast meat and hopefully approached the fire. Yoong, the woman, caught him and put him in a basket.

" 'This will do for our meal tomorrow,' she said to her husband.

"But Uncle Bôo didn't want to be eaten. He made a great fuss, shrieking more loudly than a troop of monkeys at sunrise:

" 'I am the center of the world. You exist only in my head. If you kill me you will all disappear forthwith. And the world with you. There'll be nothing left. Nothing. Only the everlasting darkness of a night without stars.'

"Of course Uncle Bôo was only making such a fuss and talking all this nonsense because he was afraid of dying. Yoong shook the basket to keep him quiet, and Boong, who was tired after the day's hunting and the ayak, fell asleep. When he woke up, the fire had gone out. The night was so dark that he believed the world had disappeared. He was frightened to death. He thought then of what Uncle Bôo had said, and begged him to restore the world. Uncle Bôo first demanded to be let out of the basket:

" 'Blow on the ashes, put some dry twigs on the embers, and I'll tell the world to come back.'

[104]

"When the flames illuminated the forest, Boong, feeling reassured, wanted to go to sleep again, but Uncle Bôo went on.

" 'I am the center of the world and you exist only in my head. If you don't want everything to disappear, give me something to eat.'

" 'I haven't anything,' Boong replied. 'Only two small rat bones. I'm hungry, too.'

"Uncle Bôo sniffed at the little bones in disgust.

" 'I'm sorry to hear that. Let me at least suckle at your wife's breast.'

"Uncle Bôo was so ravenous that he bit into Yoong's breast and devoured her heart.

" 'Your wife's dead now. She's of no further use. Cook her and we'll eat her together.'

"Boong shed many tears and obeyed. As I told you, this was when the spirits themselves had fled, abandoning mankind to the powers of evil.

"After they had eaten Yoong, Uncle Bôo was still hungry.

" 'I am the center of the world and you exist only in my head. If you don't want to disappear, let me eat one of your legs. You'll still be able to walk on the other if you use a stick.'

"Boong cried more loudly than ever, because the loss of his leg saddened him even more than the loss of his wife, but he didn't want the world to disappear.

"Uncle Bôo was still hungry. He insisted on eating the other leg and both arms, one after the other. Then, sated at last, he stretched out on his back and slept until morning.

[105]

"On waking up, he felt extremely thirsty and went down to the Sembakung, indifferent to the groans of Boong, who was unable to move. He sat down on the edge of the great river, which was now nothing more than a modest stream trickling between banks of reddish sun-baked silt, and drank so much and so deeply that he failed to notice a big muddy tree trunk floating in what remained of the water. It was only by the skin of his teeth that he avoided the terrible snapping jaws of the muddy tree trunk. Uncle Bôo had eaten too much and drunk too much to escape for long from the old crocodile, who was slavering and grunting with greed.

" 'Good morning,' he said to him. 'I've been looking for you. I've prepared you a meal.'

The wary old crocodile drew a little closer and growled, 'A good meal? There's nothing left to eat within a radius of fifty leagues. What is it?'

" 'A man.'

" 'A man?' echoed the old crocodile. 'But men run too fast, and they're as dangerous as buffaloes on the rampage.'

" 'This one won't run very far. Listen to me, O Master of the River. I've drunk too much and I've eaten too much, I'm tired. I shall climb on to your back and guide you to him.'

" 'A man!' the old crocodile exclaimed again. 'I've only eaten one in the whole of my life, but it's so long ago that I've forgotten the taste. Off we go!'

"After he had led the crocodile to Boong, Uncle Bôo jumped down and quietly disappeared into the forest.

[106]

The old crocodile, who was a gourmet, thought that Boong would taste better if he left him to marinate for some time in a hole in the river. He dragged him down.

"Boong sank into the water, weeping, and this time the world really did disappear. For him at least."

Between two ramparts of vegetation, the Sembakung glided slowly by under the stars, like a wide strip of black lacquer, without an eddy, without a wave, without a ripple, impassive, silent, dead. From time to time there was a brief gurgle, and a faint shimmer like diamond dust irradiated the polished surface: fleeting signs of life, swept away immediately afterward by the great river's invisible flight into darkness, toward its savage delta, toward the sea.

So time flowed by. Under the moist sky of morning. Under the torrid sky of noon. Under the sun of naked truth, of absolute good and evil, when everything in shade seems doomed to darkness and everything in sunlight—faded, blanched, purified—seems saved. The merciless vertical sun which already clamps a death mask on the faces of the living, by hollowing out cheeks and eye sockets with black. The great red sun of evening which bathes this shrouded earth in blood. The sky at night . . .

So our days glided by.

The relentless battering of the rain, the sinister

splendor of the jungle, banked clouds, Orion and Altair in the constellation of Aquila, the physical delights of the body, the warmth of friendship . . . Life!

Learoyd was in truth a king. During those days I saw him govern and administrate. I saw him dispense justice under a tree. I saw him give orders, for such was his pleasure. I saw him feared, admired, respected, envied. I saw him loved. By God, I can say so: I saw him King.

In his wake I followed the great valleys, made my way up torrents, skirted the blue mountain ridges. I bathed in the coolest waterholes in the Forest of the Spirits. I slept in countless villages, attended numerous palavers, a great many settlements of debts. Learoyd traveled without luggage with his escort of warriors. Everywhere he was welcomed with joy and respect. He was simple, accessible to all, even when he was often obliged to spend all night drinking and listening to stories that were enough to send you to sleep on your feet, about dragon jars, slaves, and bloodshed.

When everything was settled and sorted out, I would sometimes hear him repeat over and over again a word which he had just heard for the first time, until he pronounced it correctly and understood exactly what it meant; he would then produce his quill and bamboo inkpot and jot it down on the back of a Japanese propaganda leaflet which served as a notebook, using the phonetic writing he had invented in which the peculiar accents were represented by odd signs—little squares, circles, and triangles—which he alone understood.

[109]

Frequently he would finish the night with a young girl whose body had been "fashioned by the spirits." When I became his friend, he suggested I should marry —temporarily, for the duration of my stay—a young widow of Senghir's lineage. I refused. I was quite willing for my body to sweat and tremble with exhaustion. I was quite willing to feed it, water it. I took an animal delight in straining it, forcing it to the limit, in plunging it into the icy waters of a torrent to wash away the fatigue, sweat, and grime of a long day's march. I enjoyed the pleasure of a bowl of ayak in the evening at sundown, a cigarette at dawn when it was shiveringly cold and damp, fire after rain, rice after hunger. I even reveled in the bliss of a sound digestion after an orgy of pork and buffalo.

But the softness of a woman's body I refused. Flesh was to flesh and spirit to spirit, and I feared as a shameful weakness the moment when the two should meet. I refused tenderness.

"You talk of life, of good and evil, but you have no tenderness. That's why you're inhuman," Learoyd told me.

My body was an instrument, a slave constantly at my command. I believed that war should be chaste, I believed . . . But to hell with what I believed! The curse of the flesh! "She eateth, and wipeth her mouth, and saith, 'I have done no wickedness.'" The old inheritance!

"It was only a suggestion, you know," Learoyd went on. "It would have helped me to keep an eye on the old crow. There's nothing better than a woman's eye."

[110]

Learoyd had a special affection for the Comanche army, *his* army. He never once failed to inspect the local militias. I would then recognize in him, like an indelible stamp, the good old traditions of the British Army NCO. One day I saw him dispense justice. It was an important case as a matter of fact, because two militias, siding with their respective villages, were threatening to come to blows.

It was one of those overcast afternoons when the lowering sky presses down on the restless earth like a leaden lid, when the storm in the offing racks the nerves, and rage, hatred, and cruelty seem to prowl in the shadows like the errant spirits of the powers of evil. The wise men of the council approached the subject under discussion so deviously that I wondered how Learoyd could make head or tail of the business. Those confounded wise men took over an hour, in the muggy atmosphere of their longhouse, to come to the point. Luckily it was not yet ayak time.

"A female buffalo that was about to calve. And in the other village, the one upstream, another female buffalo in the same condition . . . But the inhabitants of the upstream village are notorious liars . . . Aagan never gave the jar he had promised as a dowry for the marriage of . . ."

Learoyd translated their incoherent statements for my benefit. He listened to these jeremiads patiently, but he was sweating, and I felt he was worried.

The long and the short of it was that one of the two newborn buffaloes had disappeared. Dead? Eaten by a

[111]

wild animal? Meanwhile both villages were laying claim
to the survivor. For the sake of a buffalo calf they were
ready to fly at each other's throats without giving
quarter. For the sake of a little buffalo that could not
have weighed more than two hundred pounds. And for
the sake of honor, I imagine, for the sake of pleasure.

Learoyd summoned the councils of the two villages
to neutral territory. He sat down under a big banyan
tree with the downstream council on one side, the upstream council on the other, each glaring angrily at the
other, and the young buffalo in the middle, calmly graz-
ing. The entire population of both villages, women and
children included, had gathered around, looking as
though they might soon be pitching into each other with
sticks and stones. Beyond lay the motionless jungle,
which seemed to wait, and above stretched the sky,
growing heavier and heavier, blacker and blacker: a
storm! I felt like settling the case myself by drawing my
Colt and shooting the blasted animal dead so that they
could share the carcass and stop talking about it.

Learoyd gave orders for the two female buffaloes to
be brought up. The little calf, which had lain down,
now sprang to its feet, startled, and gazed at us for some
time, muzzle outstretched, champing its grass blades,
shaking its ears to chase away the flies. Then it ambled
toward the upstream people and unconcernedly sniffed
at the hindquarters of its equally indifferent mother.
There was a roar of laughter; a few seconds later the
storm broke with a loud clap of thunder and a sudden
gust of whirling wind. Then the rain began to fall, as

[112]

though the powers of evil were acknowledging their defeat.

So our days glided by.

We went up as far as Tomani. I covered the last few miles barefoot in case a Japanese patrol should spot the print of my boots, which would inevitably indicate the presence of a white man, and I left a trail of blood in the mud behind me. Luckily none of my cuts festered. Through my field glasses I saw my first Japanese: a sentry outside a stone hut. He had a long rifle equipped with a long bayonet, a small peaked cap, and round spectacles. I remember him well because I could have killed him; I could have taken a rifle from one of the Comanches, lined him up in the sights, and killed him, just like that, for no reason. And if I did not do so, it was only because I was anxious not to incur the wrath of the Japanese too soon. I was surprised nevertheless to discover so much cold-blooded violence in myself. The mark of Cain!

Two trucks rattled past in the stifling heat, and the sentry disappeared in the clouds of reddish dust they had raised behind them. Around us some dogs barked.

On the way back we went by the former Japanese route up the valley of the Upper Tungkalis, winding through a maze of gorges, ramparts, ravines, pools of muddy water infested with leeches, crumbling bamboo groves, tangled thorn bushes, clinging jungle: a seething, slimy hell dominated by the magnificent and serene

[113]

forests on the mountains. Learoyd's first battlefield. The last expedition of Tamong Miri the Terrible.

In the evening we camped in a huge clearing above the river, reveling in what was for the Muruts a luxury: a cloudless sky. The Comanches roasted a wild boar and boiled rice in hollow bamboo. The night was pellucidly clear, the late afternoon rain having washed the sky clean. We were happy.

After the meal we stretched out on our backs beside the glowing embers and gazed at the stars as we nibbled blades of grass. The world was silent. We talked of distant things, of all one talks of in the starlight when happy—of friendship. I had taken out my binoculars to observe Orion and Altair more closely, and I could see other little specks of light invisible to the naked eye. And there were others still, which the most powerful telescope would not have shown. It was one of those blissful nights when one forgets that man is a passing stranger on this earth, that life, friendship, death have no more importance than the fate of the grass blades we were nibbling, that nature is neither gentle nor cruel: she is nothing.

A sheet of mist white in the moonlight rose slowly from the Tungkalis like a flood, silently inundating the valley at our feet, blotting out the ravines, engulfing the nearest trees. Learoyd flung an armful of bamboo twigs on the embers, and the leaping flames, crackling with sparks, repulsed the ghostly tide around us.

Seeing our happy faces, the Comanches chattered at the tops of their voices until dawn.

[114]

I collected seeds and dried some epiphytes and orchids for the Kew herbarium. I took notes for the
corrections to my 1936 book. I completed my documen-
tation of certain species: the banyan *(Ficus bengalensis)*,
feared and venerated by the Muruts, a monstrous vegetable octopus which strangles other trees and shatters
walls of stone, as at Borobodur and Angkor; *Antiaris
toxicaria*, which provides the poison for the arrows
whose terrifying effects on man I was shortly to witness;
Hopea odorate, Alstonia scholaris . . .

Throughout this trip I was never out of touch with
Armstrong and my Australians. Learoyd had long ago
built up a network of communications via relays of
runners day and night: a regular Pony Express (there
were even a couple of horses, captured from the Japanese, which were galloped along the bridle paths of the
Plain of Elephants). In eight days news could travel
from one side of the kingdom to the other. I learned
that Conklin and Gwai had reached the outskirts of
Tarakan without mishap, that further parachute drops
had taken place, that Fergusson was asking for information on the landing fields in the Bay of Brunei. Learoyd
went on administering his kingdom. He held long con-
ferences with his runners.

"When my tribal headmen learn to read, it'll be
easier. I'll be able to issue orders in writing."

We returned to the village. There were further parachute drops. I had a landing strip built for light aircraft
in anticipation of the invasion which would soon take

[115]

place. My mission was assuming tangible shape. We already had nearly five hundred well-trained, well-armed men available at a moment's notice; information on the Japanese kept pouring in; and I had a second radio team and transmitter for my schedules with Morotai.

Anderson was now spending his leisure hours in learning the Murut language and building a miniature three-masted schooner in a bottle of White Hart, a Japanese imitation of White Horse whiskey, which he had unearthed God knows where and shared with Truu Big-Belly-Button and his two other Comanche dynamos. He wanted to present the model to the little gray-eyed prince, whose friend he had become.

So our days glided by.

The northeasterly monsoon gradually declined, the last faint breezes circled around like caged wild beasts, building up tremendous thunderstorms. Then, little by little, a steady drift from the southwest set in, growing gradually stronger. The trade winds of the Indian Ocean set the treetops bowing to the north; they carried heavier scents, a harsher light, an atmosphere charged with indefinable forebodings.

Throughout this happy period, up to May 1, the Japanese remained decently inactive.

PART TWO

The Southwesterly Trade Winds

"Tell them of what thou alone hast seen,
then what thou hast heard . . . tell them
of battles and kings, horses, devils,
elephants and angels, but omit not to
tell them of love and suchlike."

RUDYARD KIPLING
(*Life's Handicap*)

On May 2 we heard about the fall of Berlin, but not until the 11th did we hear of Hitler's death and the capitulation of Germany. This news left us almost indifferent; it was what we had expected. The war in Europe, even though I had taken part in it, now seemed to me so distant that it had become almost alien to me. Learoyd did not want to hear anything about it. He was simply not interested. My Australians, who had been through the desert campaign, nevertheless improvised a little celebration, to the great joy of the Muruts, who are not prone to sleep and welcome any opportunity to spend all night speechifying and swigging ayak.

What remained of the war was being won far away from us. Of the two main thrusts of the Allied advance which were sweeping everything before them, one was taking place eight hundred miles away in the east, through the Philippines; the other, some two thousand miles to the northwest, through Burma, bypassing our little kingdom of jungle and rain. Borneo was merely a vague threat to MacArthur's left flank.

Neither Allied headquarters nor Fergusson had any

clear idea of what was going on beneath the vault of trees over which they had so unceremoniously dropped us. Headquarters merely wanted to ensure the security of the left flank at the lowest cost.

Fergusson was yielding to more sentimental reasons; he wanted to recover a fragment of the Empire, to render unto the Crown of England the things that were the Crown's. We were the earnest instruments of his policy. But beneath the vault of trees, in the twilight of the jungle, there was a strange spell, a charm which enthralled us once and for all; gradually the outside world —"back there," as we used to say—lost all substance and reality.

On May 1, however, "back there" had suddenly obtruded on "out here." An Australian brigade landed at Tarakan, and it was like stirring up an anthill. In the west as well as the east the Japanese got down to business and started running about in all directions, arresting notables, massacring suspects, burning down villages, terrorizing the populace. An undeclared resistance, previously vitiated by the crushing reprisals of 1944, flared up again and set the whole coastal zone ablaze.

A host of people poured into the jungle, seeking refuge. Chinese, Malays, Ibans, and Dusums abandoned their kampongs, driven out by fear, hunger, and destitution, and plunged even deeper into the interior, following the rivers and the occasional tracks. Many lost their way and died, blundering around in circles, incapable of finding their bearings in the maze of vegetation. Others were found and guided to safety by the Comanche patrols. Still others, after wandering for days on end, emerged from the forest, pale and trembling, blinking in the sunlight, and collapsed between the piles of the longhouses on the outskirts of the territory. For some time the Murut kingdom resembled a gale-lashed island whose coast is strewn with wreckage from sunken ships.

Learoyd was worried about this dismal invasion, which threatened the integrity, the proud isolation of his people. He did not want the newcomers to stay in his villages. He had camps built for them in the forest. Gwai, Senghir, all the headmen "with ears full of wisdom" likewise feared that this enforced contact with the outside world might bring about uncontrollable changes, and Learoyd knew that, once the door was ajar, it would be difficult to close it again. He felt, justifiably, that his people were not ready to confront the twentieth century, that they needed a long period of evolution in isolated conditions if they were not to degenerate like the Red Dogs into a sub-category of Malayans, ill-adapted, displaced, and dispossessed.

He was especially afraid of what would happen after the war; he feared that these refugees, who had been received out of charity, would return one day and rob the Muruts of their land. In vain did I try to tell him that his out-of-the-way kingdom was of no real interest to anyone, neither to tea planters, rubber planters, nor even prospectors, because it was too inaccessible; I failed to convince him. He seemed curiously persuaded that a horde of predators, lured by the wealth of the Domain of the Spirits, would come back and pillage it.

It was only much later, at the time of the great Battle

[121]

of the Mountain of the Dead, that I was able to account for his unreasonable concern. The Tabuk Libang river, north of the mountain, contains gold dust in its silt. Learoyd had opened a working on which he employed a score of Javanese, former auxiliaries in the Japanese army who had been taken prisoner by the Comanches. It was while wandering haphazardly up the valley that I chanced upon the outfit.

In spite of our friendship Learoyd had not mentioned it to me; he was still wary of me, wary of the diabolical fascination of gold. Yet he had seen me hand out a thousand gold sovereigns! The output of the working was paltry, and even with modern methods, the gold collected there would have cost too much to tempt anyone. But Learoyd did not know this; slowly, grain by grain of gold dust, he believed he was laying up a treasure that would help him to save his kingdom from the perils of the postwar world.

Learoyd was quite wrong to be anxious; those miserable refugees dreamed of only one thing: getting back to their paddy fields and kampongs in the deltas, back to the cool, gentle air of the coast, the brilliant colors, the great open spaces over which the eye can range with delight, the wide horizons, a clear sky, and the sea. The forest did not suit them. They felt oppressed, ill at ease. They had a constant apprehension of menace, brooding and undefined. They departed in August, as soon as the military situation would permit, turning their backs on darkness and running toward light and sun like prisoners released.

Meanwhile they bravely settled down to work, clearing patches in the jungle which were invisible from the air and growing mountain rice, tapioca, and vegetables. Nevertheless, I had to persuade Morotai to drop us some emergency supplies of rice, maize, and salt in order to avert a famine.

The Chinese are very skillful gardeners, and Learoyd arranged for three or four of these poor wretches to visit every village in his kingdom so that the Muruts might benefit from their experience and irrigation methods; one of them, overcome by loneliness, died of sheer melancholy.

My Australians took charge of the men who were capable of fighting; in a very short time there were plenty of volunteers to return to the coastal zone and establish contact with the guerrillas there. Our intelligence network thus gained further agents and, to avoid long delays in transmission, I dispatched a radio team with an armed escort to the west of the River Padas, into the northern Crockers Range which overlooks the Plain of Beaufort and the Bay of Brunei.

There was still heavy fighting in the east, round the Australian bridgehead at Tarakan. I decided to go over there and coordinate our action. In the afternoon of May 13 a light Auster aircraft picked me up on our landing strip. As the crow flies, it was no more than a hundred and fifty miles to Tarakan, but huge dark-brown clouds had gathered that day to the south of the Sembakung, and we had to make a wide detour to the east as far as the ocean, then follow the jagged coastline enveloped in mist, keeping a close watch on our petrol

[123]

gauge, only to land at nightfall, on our last drop of fuel, right in the middle of a Japanese artillery barrage.

I was warmly welcomed at Brigade headquarters. Gwai and Conklin had done a good job; their information had enabled us to sweep the Japanese air force out of the sky in a few hours and to destroy a number of ammunition dumps camouflaged in the jungle.

I quickly settled my coordination problems, and during dinner I gave an account of Learoyd, the Comanche army, and the Murut kingdom. I don't think my audience was particularly impressed. A tipsy Medical Corps colonel offered me the use of an ambulance Auster in which to evacuate my "hothead" and then embarked on a rambling explanation of the myths of Robinson Crusoe, the noble savage, and the quest for the inaccessible El Dorado, which he suddenly interrupted to push a bottle of whiskey toward me:

"Here, have some of this. Beer drinking will end by making us idiots."

The other guests showed polite interest, but I could sense the instinctive distrust of the professional soldier toward the scruffy amateur, toward disorder, adventure, and lack of discipline. For the rest of the meal the conversation was confined to the Afrika Korps, Rommel, Tobruk, Mersa Matruh, and memories of the Battle of Alamein. I felt lonely, far removed from these men of no curiosity, whose minds seemed desiccated by the terrible wind which blows from the desert of military servitude and glory.

The loquacious medical officer's whiskey and my own fatigue made me judge them unfairly. This brigade had bled and suffered on many battlefields in the last four years; it had been given a fresh objective, and it was bleeding again, still bleeding. This was the true face of war, but I could not help thinking that in our somber forests the air was fresher nonetheless.

The artillery thundered all night. Shortly before dawn I was awakened by shouts and the frantic rattle of automatic weapons; some Japanese snipers, a suicide patrol, had infiltrated our defense perimeter and were attacking the Headquarters tents.

The commotion went on until sunrise.

Toward midday I took off for Morotai with a plane-load of silent wounded. Halfway across, over the Celebes Sea, we ran into a huge static cloud like a gray beast lying in wait. The airplane was shaken and tossed about, as though an invisible hand wanted to smash it. The wounded groaned, a long, monotonous keening.

A tall gangling boy got to his feet. His hands, black with dried clots and red with fresh blood, thrust the orderly aside.

"Leave me alone," he said dully.

There was supplication in the pale eyes, sunk deep in his gaunt, haggard face. The orderly drew back in alarm. The tall gangling boy swayed backward and forward for some time. The seal of death spread over every feature except his eyes, which were now fixed straight ahead, with desperate purpose, on something mysterious.

"Leave me alone," he said again, then gave a strange gurgle and subsided slowly, like a great tree being felled.

A few twitches and faint shudders quivered in his

lanky frame. Life was still present, and suddenly there was nothing.

Somewhere in the middle of the Celebes Sea, at 1532 hours (local time) on May 14, 1945. What a long road he had traveled to reach this point, and no one knew anything about it.

On landing I discovered that another man had died on the way. He lay curled up on his side. He seemed asleep, but his open eyes did not respond to light, and his lips were twisted into a grin.

Morotai had changed a lot since my departure. It had become a comfortable base, with cinemas, clubs, strict military hierarchy, and futile interdepartmental bickering. The beaches swarmed with GIs splashing about in the water like so many New Yorkers weekending at Coney Island.

Fergusson was waiting for me at Special Forces Advanced Base.

Fergusson was the boss of our outfit. He had handpicked us and given us a training which would have been the envy of the greatest criminals in history. At the special commando school at Great Barrier Reef he had taught us, with terrifying enthusiasm, to dispatch a living creature into the next world, to steal, to destroy anything built by human hands—in short to commit every sort of evil.

After he had thus armed and armored us against a ruthless world, he sent us forth to accomplish his design: to win back a lost empire and restore it to the Crown.

His shadow hovered over our every action. He was our mentor, at once master, stern father, and "sage with big ears." On my arrival at Darwin in 1944 he had informed me:

"Never let me hear you complain of ingratitude on the part of the people on whose side you're going to fight, because it's for *your* sake you're going to suffer and maybe die, not for theirs. Don't think you're another Christ. You're a man, the latest model of a mere man."

He was tough and self-assured, his statements cut straight through like an axe.

"Real justice is injustice," he often used to say, and in fact he could be terribly unjust. We respected him, we admired him, and I don't think he ever knew how much we loved him.

There was an invisible flaw, however, in this impressive façade. The date of the great rendezvous was not so very distant: one day in October 1946, somewhere in the middle of the ocean, as it was for the tall gangling boy on the plane. But this time Death would not need to force the issue; it would merely have to bide its time in a particular spot which it alone knew.

Fergusson asked me to be seated, opened a bottle of Kentucky bourbon, and poured me out a glass. Then he produced a box of Manila cigars which some American pilots had brought back for him, offered me one, and carefully lit his own. He had the precise, methodical gestures of a schoolmaster arranging his notes, books, and pencils in front of him before examining his pupil.

"Go ahead," he said simply.

I swallowed a mouthful (whiskey, even bourbon, is decidedly better than ayak) and began by giving an account of the Comanche army guaranteed to delight the heart of an old soldier.

"We have roughly six hundred men under arms, but the size of the units varies, depending on family and tribal laws and the vagabond mood of the Muruts. In actual fact we can't count on more than five hundred warriors at any given moment.

"The Western concept of discipline, which is the

[128]

main strength of an army, doesn't make sense to them. The Muruts are free men taking part of their own free will in a war and choosing of their own free will to withdraw from it whenever it suits them. Sometimes an entire militia, in a fit of nostalgia, marches off *en masse* to spend a few days back in its valley.

"Each militia is a small autonomous group under the authority of a headman appointed by Learoyd and supported by our Australian instructors. In theory, the old tribal squabbles have been settled. In reality, any opportunity—a distribution of arms, for instance—is apt to revive enmity. It's a heterogeneous community. The Murut nation may be being forged, but it isn't yet a *fait accompli.*

"The Comanche warriors are young, between fifteen and twenty-five, though the word 'warrior' in Murut denotes any man with enough strength and courage to draw a sword. They are stark naked except for a strip of cloth around their loins and a few ornaments of copper, ivory, and calao quills. They can exist indefinitely in any jungle on a handful of berries and bamboo shoots, lie in wait without moving a muscle for a wild animal or an enemy, kill soundlessly and disappear without trace. They are fascinated by lethal weapons and destructive devices. They look after their rifles with loving care and are even capable of carrying out complicated repairs on their improvised forges.

"To sum up, they're a superb army for defensive action, deception, and ambush. Mediocre, if not worse, in attack. Useless, probably, in any terrain except their own. Incapable of suffering heavy losses—a defeat entailing many casualties would so horrify them that the tribes would fade away into the jungle." (This had actually happened to Learoyd on the Upper Tungkalis.) "An army after my own heart, for whom warfare is an individual joy and not a dismal collective butchery.

"In my opinion we should arm them only with light weapons, such as the M-1 American carbine, and explosives for booby traps. Thus equipped, they would be able to hold the interior indefinitely while the 9th Australian Division in the coastal zone could deal with the Japanese being harassed in the rear."

I then elaborated on my theory of submarine warfare. Like every civilian, I took a particular pleasure in dabbling in the art of war. I had of course studied Hannibal and Napoleon, read Clausewitz and other authorities (Mao Tse-tung was not known at that time). The role of the great captain, the victorious man of war who reverts to his plough when the empire has no more need of him, always played a vague part in the panoply of dreams that had survived my childhood.

Fergusson listened to me, puffing away at his cigar. He did not ask many questions as he studied the map corrected by Learoyd. In the end he demanded straight out:

"Tell me about your mad Irishman."

I was both expecting and dreading this question. My opinion of Learoyd had undergone considerable revision since my first encounter with him, when I had struggled to my feet out of the mud, trembling with rage, but it was by no means conclusive. I was still of two minds

[130]

about him, but Learoyd was there; I was making use of him; I still believed I had him under control.

I gave a rough description of him, adding a few anecdotes to enhance it, then told Fergusson about my doubts.

"I don't think the situation is as simple as our Australian friends at the Tarakan bridgehead think: we win the war and everything goes back to normal. No! I believe the irruption of the Japanese, and now of us, into that isolated world bypassed by progress has caused a profound upheaval. It's a new age beginning for the Muruts, as revolutionary as the discovery of iron or fire. Nothing will ever be the same again, and the Domain of the Spirits won't be able to remain outside history.

"The Muruts sense it, instinctively, incoherently, even though they're incapable of expressing it. They have felt the need to join forces. They have tolerated a foreigner—because I believe Learoyd is still a foreigner to them—so they have tolerated a foreigner piloting them on these unknown waters to help them to round the dangerous cape. Only five or six years ago they would have cut off his head without a moment's hesitation.

"I'm not sure they've made a bad choice. Learoyd is also one of them. He loves them. I don't think he'll ever abandon them. I don't quite understand why. Perhaps he's afraid of the rest of the world? Or is it his way of rebelling? Rebelling against—I don't know—life? The world? Perhaps it's much simpler. Is he happy? Yes, he *is* happy!"

[131]

Fergusson sank back in his armchair and vanished behind a cloud of cigar smoke.

"You say he's king?"

When I did not reply, he picked up an envelope on his desk and tossed it across to me.

"Have a look at this."

It contained a police report on Learoyd, extracts from his personal file, and statements from his officers. I learned that he had been born in 1919 (so he was twenty-six, four years younger than I was) in County Tyrone. His parents were humble tenant farmers. At the age of sixteen he went to stay with an aunt in Belfast and worked first as a delivery boy for a brewery, then in a shipbuilding yard. In 1938, with a gang of youths of his own age, he took part in several terrorist actions: raids on a barracks at night, the wrecking of a Catholic pub, thefts from the docks, etc. In the course of a street fight there was a fatal casualty: an injured policeman who died in the hospital. Shortly afterward Learoyd was arrested and sentenced to five years in prison.

Released at the outbreak of war, his sentence having been commuted, he joined the army and was posted to the Far East. His officers' reports gave a scarcely better impression: an average soldier, a crack shot with a Bren gun. By 1941 he had nevertheless risen to the rank of sergeant but showed little authority. It was in action, during the retreat from Perak, that he finally proved his worth. Cut off by the Japanese advance, he succeeded three weeks later in rejoining his company on the River Slim, with very few casualties and his full complement of weapons. In February he was reported missing at the time of the fall of Singapore.

In the bottom of the envelope there was also a photograph. A wretched little slum kid with a sharp, strained, ferrety face: Learoyd on the day he was sent to prison. I would never have recognized him. I wouldn't have relied for a second on this shifty-eyed youth. I would certainly never have bestowed one of my gold sovereigns on him.

I handed the papers back to Fergusson without saying a word. He was still puffing at his cigar, but his eyes never left me.

"In this war," he said, after a long silence, "there are many people who have lost everything, their friends, their worldly goods, their lives and, what is worse, their honor, their dignity. War doesn't sentimentalize. I'm not asking you if your Irishman is a good fellow and if you like him. That doesn't interest me. The Murut kingdom doesn't exist. There's North Borneo, the Sultanate of Sarawak, and the Dutch Colony.

"If your Irishman believes he's a king, then he's mad. And if you believe in his fantasy, then you're mad. As mad as he is. We're no longer in the nineteenth century. The days when Brook could," he went through the motion of snatching something from his desk, "are over.

"I'm afraid you had a hard landing, like that wretched Sergeant Simson—no, Simpson—Simson or Simpson. To hell with him anyway! Do you know he refused to salute me, the blighter, he refused to salute anyone.

[133]

"So far as I can see from your poor devil's map, he's built himself a private kingdom astride three frontiers. That's all! What's Rajah Brook going to say about it, eh? Not to mention the Dutch. They're going to think the Intelligence Service, or God knows who, are up to some monkey business behind their backs."

I was furious with Fergusson's remarks. I had the feeling I was contending, as at Tarakan, with lassitude, indifference, blindness. For all Fergusson's intelligence, he had not understood a word of what I had told him.

I replied curtly, "You sent me to the Muruts. I dropped by parachute. And this is what I found—a king. I don't believe this or that, I'm not inventing, I'm not dreaming, I'm not off my head. I've only tried to show you how and why he has been able to become king. The first time I saw him I could have killed him, now he's my . . . But that's neither here nor there. No! I've merely been trying to tell you that after the war things won't just revert to normal."

Fergusson interrupted me.

"Don't get excited. I know all about that. I know. I wanted to give you a word of advice, to tell you something about your poor—about your friend. You see, I know this sort of set-up. It always ends disastrously—in shabby failure. He'd have done better to chuck himself into the sea when his ship was torpedoed, with his pockets stuffed with ammunition to make sure he sank at once. One day he'll be sorry he ever came to Borneo. And if you get too deeply involved with him, you'll be sorry too."

Fergusson was making an effort to smile, but his

eyes remained serious and sad. I looked at him in amazement. He had never talked like this before. He was un-
sure of himself, something had broken. I looked away,
embarrassed by his emotion. I felt it was indecent to see
a man's eyes suddenly reflect his essence, his soul, like a
woman's eyes in the act of love. Such moments are few
and far between, thank heavens. Our body is an opaque
envelope, and our soul remains invisible.

"To devote one's life to—no, I mean to let oneself
be possessed by another race is sheer delusion. It's sell-
ing one's soul to the devil. A renegade. There's no
greater curse than being a renegade. Being a deserter,
perhaps? The devil can't be reckoned with. One fine day
you have to betray one or other of them. You daren't go
home again, ever. Or else you try and drown it all in
drink—too disgusting!

"Mind you, you can build them roads, teach them to
build roads, bridges, anything you like. You can bring
them law and order, justice, education—come to them
with hands outstretched, saying: 'I'm your friend.' You
can even learn something from them. But you must stay
British. It's not contempt. It's—a line of conduct. You're
not one of them, you never will be. You're no longer one
of us either, you're a dead leaf. I can tell you from personal experience, I . . ."

He gazed at his cigar and carefully snuffed it out in
the ashtray.

"No! You've got to stay British," he declared with
force.

At the time I was relieved he did not embark on
personal experiences—yet another of those horrible war

memories. Today I regret it, for it might have shed a gleam of light on the reasons for his suicide.

Fergusson rose to his feet, as though he had suddenly recovered all his self-assurance.

We went off for a swim. The GIs had returned to their barracks. We were alone on a beach littered with empty cigarette packets and old newspapers. The sea was deep purple tinged with slate-gray reflections. A huge somber red sun was sinking slowly in the misty glory of dusk. It was very beautiful, but there was a sort of nagging despair in the day's death agony, and I did not feel the joy I expected at the sight of the immense, open, unrestricted horizon to which all the Muruts aspire.

"It's the best time of day, there's never anyone here," said Fergusson.

I swam with him for ten minutes in the phosphorescent water; then I left him and made my way back to the shore, which was barely visible in the gathering darkness. The current must have swept me off my course, for I landed more than three hundred yards away from our jeep and had some difficulty in finding it. I was worried about Fergusson. When I left him he had been swimming strongly out to sea, toward the last mysterious glimmer of daylight. Now sky, earth, and water were merged into the same opaque darkness, limitless and fathomless, dank as a tomb. Two miles to the north I could see the luminous haze of the air base; a dying land breeze gusted fitfully and the roar of aircraft reached my ears.

I tried to shout, but my cries sounded ridiculous. A distant lightning flash showed up heavy storm clouds, then was extinguished silently. I turned the jeep toward the sea and signaled with the headlights.

A long time afterward, Fergusson staggered out of the water and, dripping wet, climbed into the jeep's driver's seat.

"Worrying, this Learoyd business. Very worrying!"

Two cars came racing up to us and drew up with a squeal of brakes. The beam of a portable spotlight blinded us.

"Was it you signaling out to sea?" a voice barked.

Fergusson explained who he was to the military police, one of whom came cautiously forward. I was aware of the others, still on the alert, prowling around us.

"I'll have to report you, sir."

Fergusson grunted an acknowledgment and produced his documents. The MP spread them out on the hood of the jeep to examine them. From one of the vehicles came the buzz of a radio transmitter; a voice announced a call sign, then gave our particulars:

". . . a jeep . . . Two Englishmen in underpants . . . No! Ha! Ha! Ha! They say they've been swimming! One of them's a colonel . . ."

Fergusson lit a cigar. He looked deeply concerned. He put his hand on my shoulder and muttered with unusual emotion: "Tell him to come back."

I looked at him in amazement. Then I realized he was referring to Learoyd.

"He won't," I said.

"Good Christ! Put the fear of God into him, threaten

[137]

him with a court-martial! He's still a bloody sergeant, damn it!"

The MP looked up in surprise from his notebook: "Did you say something, sir?"

Fergusson gave an exasperated shrug: "No. Have you finished with us now?"

The MP handed back his papers. The spotlight suddenly went out. There was a roar of engines revving up. The two vehicles described a semicircle, sweeping the darkness with their headlights, then raced off, pitching and swaying over the bumpy track. Fergusson sat without moving. A faint red glow was reflected in his eyes each time he drew on his cigar.

We drove back in silence. Shortly before reaching Special Forces Advanced Base we passed an open-air cinema just as a killer in a black hat, cigarette dangling from his lips, was firing his revolver. The shots rang out with the same violence as at Tarakan. A man bit the dust. A woman screamed and flung herself on the body, embracing it, sobbing. Her lamentations pursued us for some time.

"You really need him?" Fergusson asked me as we drew up.

I was about to reply and repeat all my arguments again, but he forestalled me:

"Yes, of course," he muttered listlessly.

Fergusson was still thinking about Learoyd. He knew him only from the police photograph of a pasty-faced slum kid, from statements in a police report and from the vague picture I myself had painted, which gave no indication, apart from a distant echo muffled by successive reverberations, of the true nature of the King of the Muruts. Yet this distant echo had been sufficiently powerful to reveal his gruff sentimentality.

Today I am convinced, without the slightest evidence, that there was some subtle connection between Learoyd and Fergusson's suicide. I cannot say exactly what. It would have needed so little, on that warm evening in the Halmaheras—a little human tenderness, an affectionate glance, a word—for Fergusson to speak and lift a corner of the veil. But I was too preoccupied with myself at the time. Reading through my diary, I find nothing but my daydreams, anxieties, doubts, and uncertainties, an endless conversation with myself, the reflection of a self-satisfied egocentricity, as though the world war, Borneo, the jungle, the death of others, existed only to help me acquire a better knowledge of myself.

So I remained distant as I sat in the jeep—not really distant—how shall I put it? Neutral, that's it. And today Fergusson's behavior remains as much of an enigma to me as the picture I glimpsed on that open-air screen: the murder of a man and the scream of a woman.

When we had gone swimming together at sundown, I had left Fergusson and swum back to shore because I was frightened. The sea, the darkness, filled me with an irrational anguish. Of course there were also sharks, but they did not count for much beside the nightmares engendered by my imagination. I made for the land because I was seized with panic, and Fergusson knew nothing of it.

So what do I know of Fergusson? What does one ever

know of a man? What do I know of my own father? On some evenings there was such distress in his gaze. His eyes—and I turned aside. The rest of the time he appeared hopelessly fuddled. He died in his bed, like the wounded man on the plane. Not the tall gangling boy who got to his feet, refused all help and, all alone, watched death approach. No, like the other one, who died in his sleep. Choked by his own vomit.

What do I know of my father? Only that he loved me!

"Tell him . . ."

Fergusson took a final puff at his cigar and tossed it away. The glowing butt described an arc in the night and died in a brief burst of sparks.

"No, nothing."

What had he wanted to say? Was it a message? A call for help? A warning? A mark of friendship?

I don't know.

Two days later I left Morotai in the gentle breeze of dawn. I was taking with me two fresh radio teams and supplies for my refugees. The sky was paling in the east while the mechanics warmed up the engines of the Liberator. We drank a last cup of coffee in the pilots' mess. The light turned gray, pink, then suddenly pale sparkling gold as the sun appeared. The air had the freshness and briskness of a summer holiday morning in England.

I was glad to be leaving Morotai.

In front of me, beyond the steely-glinting Celebes Sea, lay Borneo, the citadel of a free people, of Learoyd. The savage heart of life.

Toward eleven o'clock the pilot drew my attention to something on the horizon that looked like a cloud.

"The black widow," he said laconically.

At a height of fourteen thousand feet the jagged outline of Mount Kinabalu was emerging from the heat mist with startling clarity, like a mirage floating in the vast expanse of light. I remembered the bare black rock, the steep slopes covered in somber forests glimpsed through the gray clouds of the northeasterly monsoon a few months before; I remembered the butterflies in my stomach, the dryness in my mouth and my leap into the unknown. Now everything was different; I was coming home in high spirits, full of projects, like a countryman returning from town to the familiar surroundings of his little village.

The aircraft lost height, skirted the Sembakung, invisible beneath a river of white mist, veered to the east and flew up our valley; the speed of the engines decreased, the jungle's curly pelt flashed past very close to the aperture, then the bright green of the paddy fields, and I jumped.

I landed in the midst of an uproar.

Armstrong briefed me at once: in the stream of refugees from the west coast there were two missionary fathers, Portuguese half-castes from Timor, who promptly decided to evangelize the Muruts. Learoyd was furious and had had them arrested in my absence. He intended to expel them from the territory under armed guard.

"I won't have my people bullied by priests," he proclaimed vehemently. "I know what the Papists are like, I know only too well. Besides, they're dirty-minded brutes, they see the flesh and the devil everywhere. If I let them have their way they'd insist on all the girls wearing bras and panties. No, I won't have it!"

The two prisoners were expected that evening.

"A nasty business," Armstrong growled, "a nasty business. There are quite a lot of Christians among the refugees. We can't allow this sort of thing."

[142]

He was absolutely right, but I knew Learoyd could be pigheaded and quick tempered—that damned Irish nature of his—and I didn't want to clash with him head on. I was also curious to see how things would work out. I moved down from my command post midway to the radio station and went to spend the night in the longhouse with several bottles of Kentucky bourbon and a box of Manila cigars that Fergusson had given me when I took off.

The two missionaries and their Comanche escort arrived late at night. They were two skinny little men, with the gray complexion and hollow cheeks of medieval saints. They were worn out, obviously ill, and pitiful to look at in their threadbare sweat-stained cassocks.

They had wandered for weeks in the green gloom of tunnel-like tracks to escape the Japanese. They had faced up to the terrors of the jungle and the dark. Some of their comrades in misfortune had stopped, groaning with misery, and lain down to die; others had silently dropped in their tracks; still others had given up and retraced their steps, laughing heartily to conceal the shame they felt at their own faintheartedness. These two had humbly plodded on. They had reached the borders of the kingdom, they had believed it was a haven of mercy, and they had given thanks to Our Lord. They had proclaimed to the Muruts that fifteen thousand miles away, and almost two thousand years ago, a man had been nailed to a cross to redeem their sins and on the third day had risen from the dead *ad majorem*

[143]

Dei gloriam! Then, one morning, the Comanches had snatched them from their flock and dragged them along here.

They had their hands tied behind their backs, like criminals. At a signal from Gwai they were released forthwith. They sat down, rubbing their fingers to restore the circulation.

I watched Learoyd; this was certainly not the adversary he had been preparing to confront all this evening. He said nothing; his steely eyes were as inscrutable as ever, but the atmosphere in the longhouse had undergone a sudden change.

We had drunk a great deal and smoked a great deal while waiting. Learoyd had been particularly merry; the prospect of settling an old score must have pleased him. He had told us the local legend of the creation of the world, which bears a curious resemblance to the Book of Genesis. The parable of the first sacrifice: how the evil spirits whispered slyly to men to offer to the invisible powers, in gratitude, their most precious possession: their own blood; how, on seeing this, the good spirits quickly dispatched a messenger to try to save mankind from the curse and to tell them to immolate buffaloes, not human beings; and how, in the course of the ritual meal that followed the ceremony, some of the guests unwittingly ate buffalo meat that had been dipped in the blood of the first human victim, so that they and their descendants were thus stamped with the mark of violence and cruelty. The story of the Flood, too, when the first man built a big bamboo raft and took all the animals aboard, the tiger and the buffalo, the

[144]

elephant and the ant, the scorpion and the frog. And how they forgot the duck, which swam behind them with a hen on its back.

The atmosphere had altered with the arrival of the two specters of God. I think we all felt slightly ashamed on Learoyd's behalf. Gwai sat squatting on his haunches, as impassive as a Buddha. Armstrong, Corbett, Anderson, and I were waiting. The silence was strained, something was going to happen. The younger of the two priests stood motionless, stooping slightly, looking at Learoyd; his eyes, sunken and dark-circled, melancholy as a monkey's, wrung one's heart.

Learoyd still said nothing. There was a great gust of wind, and it started to rain. Slow, heavy, steady rain, monsoon rain, flood rain. One felt it might go on raining like this for forty days and forty nights, or for the seven years of the Murut legend.

"Our Lord be with you," the young priest said at last, in English.

Learoyd passed his hand over his eyes. The flames gleamed on his tattoo mark and accentuated the rib bones of his skinny chest, which was glistening with sweat. He looked to me as pitiful as his victims.

"I don't want you to go around preaching, filling my Muruts with your claptrap," he said rudely.

"Are you afraid of the word of God?"

"None of that nonsense! My Muruts have their spirits and they're happy. They don't need your God, or your Devil."

Thus began a surprising duel between two wraiths of men, an impossible dialogue between one who be-

[145]

lieved in life everlasting and the remission of sins, and one who refused to believe. The clear sunlit side and the fearful somber side of the same quest for . . . for . . . call it what you will, the reason of life, dignity, even God.

The older priest uttered only one sentence, shaking his head rather sadly, "Pride! The son of the morning, Satan himself, succumbed to it, dragging with him in his fall a third of the celestial legions."

The rain continued to fall with a regular, nerve-racking patter. Scraps of sentences come back to my mind, glimpses of faces in the orange torch-light, eyes watching, the sound of voices. The young priest with the sad eyes spoke in a low, monotonous tone, without ever raising his voice. Learoyd mastered his feelings. He must have been furious with himself, like a man who has run headfirst into a trap.

"I know what you people are like," he said exasperatedly, "but my Muruts don't. I have to protect them."

"God has set before every man a doorway that none can close."

"Well, I'm closing it now. God, out!" Learoyd interrupted hoarsely.

His cheeks were flushed with rage.

It all seemed too absurd, like an anticlerical demonstration in Hyde Park at the turn of the century, the same threadbare catchwords. But the words were not important—neither of these two ghosts really knew how to express himself—the thing was what lay behind the words: the darkness in which men struggle, their anxieties, their eternal questions. The first time I saw him, Learoyd had told me that he had besought God to help him when he was alone in the jungle, that he had even challenged Him and cried out:

"I've done more than my share. Now it's up to You."

It was all too absurd; here we were, at war with Japan, and these two poor devils—forgive the expression—were having a set-to about God! Armstrong shot me a despairing glance. Learoyd was going to expel the two missionaries, as he had threatened, and we were going to have serious trouble with the Christian refugees. With the others as well, moreover. The splendid anti-Japanese unanimity, the cloudless cooperation with the Sino-Malayan resistance on the coast—all that was over. Over and done with! Pride: the old priest with the sorrowful face was right. Learoyd was crazed with pride, and he was going to drag us down with him in his fall.

Yes, Learoyd was proud, but he was a king, he knew how to govern. All of a sudden his anger evaporated, and he said calmly, concisely, "I had decided to have you escorted to the Dayaks down south, because I don't want you here. But you're in no state to make the journey. If I send you there you'll die on the way."

"Death is a certainty for all of us," the young priest promptly replied in his gentle voice. "The only uncertainty is the precise day and hour of our death. But it is known to God from all eternity."

Learoyd smiled bitterly.

"Let me speak. I'm going to give you the chance to choose between life and death. If you stay quiet, if you don't try to convert my Muruts, I'll keep you here like any other refugee. If not . . ." He gave a shrug.

"That's all I have to say. Drink, eat, and go to sleep.

[147]

Tomorrow you'll give me your answer. I don't want to hear anything more tonight—anger is a bad counselor."

With these words Learoyd rose to his feet. He picked up a torch and, followed by Gwai, disappeared into the darkness of the longhouse. Armstrong heaved a sigh of relief. No one uttered a word until the two black silhouettes, outlined against the orange glow from the flame, had vanished behind a bamboo partition.

I found Learoyd's suggestion perfectly reasonable, but the young priest with the sad eyes evidently thought differently. His voice rose, gentle and firm, in the silence, "Let us eat and drink, brethren, for tomorrow we die."

He really had the vocation of a martyr. Armstrong and I had great difficulty in persuading him to choose life—not for long, even so, for the poor fellow died two weeks later from exhaustion and lassitude, despite Corbett's ministrations. The old priest, on the other hand, had his soul riveted to his body; he endured the whole campaign. Perhaps he is still alive? He said to us that night, "I'm fond of life. I expect nothing from death, apart from the mercy of Our Lord."

His companion's intransigent attitude made him smile, a smile full of benevolence and understanding which seemed to illuminate his granite countenance from within.

"Youth! Cruel youth. You must forgive the young, they don't see colors as we do, to them everything is either black or white. But man happens to be gray. Ha! Ha! Ha!"

His stony mask gave way before his bitter laugh:

[148]

"They're very much alike, those two. But we are only men, aren't we? Only men—that's to say, gray. But those two want to be in the image of God. They're children."

He worked with exemplary devotion in the hospital organized by a refugee doctor, a Hokkien Chinese from Beaufort. A very remarkable man was Dr. Cheng—or Chang, I don't remember which. He had been educated in Singapore and knew the whole coastline of the South China Sea—"our Mediterranean" he used to call it.

"The dragon jars you see everywhere are Chinese, some of them date back to the Tang Dynasty, twelve centuries ago. We used to exchange them for swallows' nests in our trading counters on the west coast."

His entire family had been massacred by the Japanese after the failure of the "Double Tenth," the revolt headed by Dr. Kwok in October 1943. A price had been put on his head: three or four thousand dollars, I believe. He came to us at the end of May in a pitiful condition—the forest had ruined his nerves—and at once volunteered to organize this hospital. Subsequently, when we had some wounded Japanese prisoners, he always treated them with the utmost conscientiousness. He used to say that Learoyd . . .

But what does it matter what he used to say? It's too late.

Next morning the question of the missionaries was finally settled, but it had already lost all interest for us.
During the night, that same night when Learoyd was
driving out God, Conklin announced by radio that the
Japanese had abandoned the investment of Tarakan to
a thin screen of covering troops and were massing on
the Sembakung. Patrols were moving upriver and seiz-
ing every available vessel.

This was the first premonitory sign of the dismal
tragedy that was about to befall Learoyd's kingdom, the
first warning shot, the first growl of distant thunder, the
first hollow roll of drums proclaiming the period of
madness and despair.

O vulnerable men of dust and blood, naked men
huddled around your fires, men of little consequence in
the memory of the world; O free people of the forgotten
forests beyond the great red rivers, beyond the valleys
of oblivion, behind the hills; O trackers, poison-distillers,
head-hunters, men of the rain and the wind, men of the
darkness; O heirs to the accursed creatures who drank
the blood of the first victim at the feast of the creation

of the world: the time of the powers of evil is at hand. The hunt is on. Kill! Kill! Kill!

The long retreat, the long death march of the formidable Japanese infantry is beginning; step by step, heavily, in the grim silence of soldiers in column, the cold clink of weapons, the mud slowly trodden underfoot, the darkness, the fear, the hunger—hunger already—and the everlasting rain.

The death agony of the Japanese army in Borneo was long and lingering. It lasted four months, until October. It was as sad as the sinking of a great ship. Long columns of men plunged into the fetid, sultry jungle like murderers at bay and wandered blindly without ever seeing the sky, without ever being able to light a fire. Day after day, night after night, continually, for four months, they were assailed by a horde of invisible demons. Whole groups were wiped out by the bullets of the Comanches or were blown to bits on their booby traps; some, maddened with rage, launched screaming into attacks upon the void; others kept watch, firing at shadows and phantoms.

Yet this was nothing; soon the survivors were to envy the fate of their comrades who had been killed at the outset.

There were poisoned arrows, like cold, smooth bamboo daggers in living flesh; there were those who died in dreadful agony, those who fell behind mumbling incoherently, and were gradually overtaken and abandoned; those who went mad. It was still nothing.

There was Hunger. Hunger and its train of horrors: loose and bleeding bowels, falling teeth, swollen limbs, festering sores, gangrene, unspeakable filth and deranged minds. Its victims ate weeds, leeches, insects, mud.

Nothing. It was still nothing.

Then there was Anger, murderous fury. They took a village by surprise and an absolute orgy of cruelty followed . . . who would have thought a young child to have had so much blood in him? They fled horror-stricken at discovering that they had plumbed the lowest depths of human nature. Yet they had still not seen everything. Some of those wretches had swallowed raw paddy; their stomachs swelled and burst.

Next came Despair, with the abominable buzzing of the flies which announces death as surely as a flock of vultures. They groaned, they whimpered, cursed and shouted. They implored. The tracks were dotted with bodies hanging from the trees, the valleys rang with isolated shots.

Help! Help!

It was not yet finished, the worst was yet to come. Happy the weaklings who had the wisdom to kill themselves, for those still living were now to kill one another for food.

Such was the destruction of the Japanese army in Borneo. The accumulation of all the tears, all the terrors, all the agonies of thousands and thousands of men.

For me, for us, this same period was as thrilling as a cavalry charge.

May God forgive us!

[152]

A cavalry charge—what better comparison? We had been motionless and waiting; a touch of the spurs launched us forward. The tremendous movement gradually gathered momentum, an impersonal, collective exaltation from which all egoism was miraculously and temporarily absent. War relieved us of the worries of life. Grim waves of pride at times broke over us to see in what despite we held our flesh, and at the same time great flames of joy enwrapped us, so intently did we feel ourselves alive. We were nothing but an elemental force in action, like fire, like the sea at the time of the great equinoctial tides. Yes, a cavalry charge! Heroic and brutal.

I still have, deeply stamped on my memory, a host of scattered but fantastically clear impressions. Warfare. A cry. Cries, and more cries, calls for help. The rain, the cold at dawn. The hideous clatter of bullets. The smells of charred wood, death, and gunpowder; the smell of flowers too, sickly sweet like corpses. Desperate bugle calls. Eyes, and eyes meeting eyes. Flashes of cowardice. Joy, terrible joy, and sudden tearless despair. Intervals

[153]

of silence. Cigarettes shared. The muddy ground in which one sank, the smell of mud. Insects with bluish wing-cases like gun metal, and flies. The abominable buzzing of the flies.

We were a barbaric, joyful horde. We were defending the Kingdom of the Three Forests, but we would have fought for the Devil himself in our aggressive desire to be victors. Our hands were red with blood; we were implacable, ruthless, indifferent to suffering and death. We were alive, and our souls sang. We were mad.

So much excess consumed our energy, and the end of the campaign, like a wave receding, left us stranded on the white sands of Victory, dazed and despondent, obscurely happy to be alive, lonely, lost in the mists of a vague and unaccountable melancholy.

This marked the apogee of Learoyd's kingdom. Then began the decline and the fall.

After the missionary question had been settled, we decided to move our command post farther east, to Tamong Miri's village, so as to be closer to the fighting. We took with us Bren, Corbett, and a radio team under the command of Anderson. All the militias who were not on guard on the western frontiers were given orders to make for the Lower Sembakung by forced marches.

A wave of optimism carried us away. Learoyd was in high spirits. He tried to poke fun at the austere and chilly young priest (who was already dying) and kept winking at me behind his back.

Four days later we reached Tamong Miri by way of tracks over splendidly wooded mountain ridges *(Calo-*

phyllum, Eugenia, Dacryodes), Falcon Peak, and the Pass of Monkeys. The lonely valley, hemmed in on all sides by a mighty forest to which shreds of mist still clung, looked melancholy and disturbing in the rain: a Chinese wash-drawing executed by an artist accursed.

We skirted the River Srai, flowing black and limpid, deep and calm between two roaring rapids, as far as the ruins of the longhouse destroyed in 1943. The dogs' barking guided us the rest of the way.

The news was good. Conklin had successfully directed, by radio, several attacks by Beaufighter bombers on the concentrations of shipping. The red Sembakung swept down dead bodies and all sorts of debris, like a river in spate, and the crocodiles in the delta were having a feast. From now on the Japanese would have to advance on foot. Excellent!

On the following day we set off to the east with a militia to reinforce Conklin. The flight of an eagle at sunrise and the roar of a stag somewhere up on Falcon Peak almost stopped us; the Comanches interpreted this as a sign from the spirits, an interdict that none might infringe. Learoyd harangued his people in no uncertain terms, and order was restored; throughout the campaign we had no more trouble of this sort.

We made our way down the Srai as far as the Sembakung and embarked on some pirogues laden with explosives. At dusk on the second day a faint breeze succeeded the stifling heat. The pitch-black night seemed heavy with omens. We glided soundlessly over a lake of oil, and imagination carried us faster still toward the unknown regions where the Japanese army was fighting.

Sometimes huge shapes brushed past us; sometimes a menacing roar announced the approach of rapids, and the pirogue, lashed by spray and buffeted by swirling waters, shot forward like a black arrow amid the fury of a tempest; then suddenly everything was calm again, smooth, silent, motionless.

Nonexistent.

Toward midnight it started to rain. A shot rang out nearby; the echo rolled for some time, reverberating from bank to bank with the violence of a riposte. Our oarsman replied with a loud cry: "Ihoy!" A tall flame flickered for a brief moment, creating a cavern of pale light in the dripping forest. A patrol was on watch. There were further shouts, a long burst of merry laughter, then everything vanished behind us in the darkness.

About two hours later we landed. It was still raining.

As soon as we entered the forest I became virtually blind and had to cling to the shoulder of the invisible Comanche in front of me. The going was frightful. The ground was pitted with muddy potholes, obstructed by inextricable tangles of briar, blocked by slippery landslides.

A ghostly dawn broke, more disheartening even than usual. The mosquitoes and midges became utterly unbearable; my face was so swollen with bites I could scarcely open my eyes. The rain persisted; the dark monotonous clouds accumulated above our heads by the southwesterly trade winds broke up heavily into a tow-

[156]

like sky which we were unable to see. We were in the
marshy savannah of the Plain of Elephants, covered in
inexorable virgin forest, fascinating to a botanist because
of the wealth of the vegetation, the variety, develop-
ment, and distribution of species, but inhuman even for
a Murut.

The matrix of the world.

Original life engendering perpetual death, fecunda-
tion, fruition, and fermentation. A tangle of creepers
dripping with sap, of fleshy leaves, slimy bark, rubbery
tentacles bristling with thorns. A greenish, sultry, feverish atmosphere saturated with nauseating stenches,
stagnating like still water under the vault of great petrified trees. Life and death intertwined in a frantic and
repugnant copulation. How can one not be appalled?

Insects: hostile, hard-shelled, glittering, brittle; the
atrocious activity of their claws. Columns of red soldier
ants, the awe-inspiring discipline of those columns.
Leeches, deaf and sightless, slowly ingesting streams of
warm blood.

The Japanese army from Tarakan was here somewhere. Thanks to Conklin, Learoyd's Comanches, and
the Royal Australian Air Force, it would mark time
here, in this accursed plain, for a whole month and be
morally and physically shattered by the time it finally
reached the borders of the kingdom: the first mountain
ridges where a breath of wind stirred.

D. M. Conklin—Dynamite Dave or Mad Dave, as
they called him at Great Barrier Reef—had just re-

[157]

turned, in high spirits and covered in mud, from a raid along the Japanese tracks when we finally reached the camp.

"I've been preparing the ground for them," he said laconically.

He was a big boisterous fellow who thought that any human problem could be solved by an appropriate charge of high explosive. He had had no difficulty in converting the Muruts to his philosophy, and together, day by day, they invented booby traps of an increasingly diabolical nature. Conklin's ambition was to "bring off a series, like a break in billiards." The comparison was his own. By this he meant that by starting with an initial trap and predicting the reactions of the Japanese soldiers, he ought to be able to make them fall logically into a series of linked disasters, each explosion producing an enemy reaction which in its turn would initiate a further explosion, and so on. After setting his first trap he would stop to think for a moment, with a frown on his face; then he would leap forward, climb and run in all directions, going through the probable motions of his future victims.

Unfortunately his cunning schemes were frustrated for some time because the Japanese advanced behind a screen of Javanese auxiliaries, led by Sikhs armed with sticks, who fled in panic at the slightest danger.

"Oh, they blow themselves up all right, but it's not a good job," Conklin would mutter, disappointed.

It was only much later, when the Japanese had exhausted their supplies of Javanese, that his perseverance was at last rewarded. He brought off one particular "break of six" which could not have been more spectacular or lethal.

I had brought him my last bottle of bourbon and several tins of corned beef. In his joy he exclaimed:

"It's paradise here, if it weren't for these bloody mosquitoes and leeches. Honestly, it's paradise."

He lived with his desperadoes, his "desert rats," and his transmitter in some huts made of foliage three hours' march (a scant two miles in the jungle) from the spearhead of the Japanese advance, but "with my little firecrackers, it'll take them at least two days, and they'll be hanging in shreds from the trees." In a very short time he had mastered a score of Murut key words which he punctuated with bloodcurdling oaths to make himself understood more clearly, and the result was remarkable. His only worry, apart from his supply of anti-personnel mines, plastic detonators, and corned beef, was the disappearance in the south of a strong Japanese column of which the Comanches had lost all trace.

"Just like that! Crossed off the Army List, you might say. But we've seen that before, it's an old Afrika Korps trick. One fine day they'll come down on us from the rear," he told me.

As it was getting late, he pushed the bottle of bourbon toward me, "If you like, we'll drink the last of it to the health of the good old 9th Division, which has taught us a trick or two, and afterward we'll go to sleep as peacefully as babes."

During the night there was an alarm. We filed out

furtively, each with a glowworm attached to his back so as not to lose one another; Conklin always kept a box full of them, which he fed on banana leaves.

Short panting bursts of Sten-gun fire, dominated by the harsh rattle of Japanese rifles, broke the silence. The darkness was so intense and the forest so thick that I couldn't see a thing, except the confounded little glow-worm flashing in front of my eyes. There were some yells and loud explosions, then suddenly a long scream of pain that chilled our blood. I bumped into the man ahead of me; we tumbled together into an oily pool of evil-smelling mud; those behind tripped over our en-tangled bodies and fell, grunting hoarsely. We lay flat on the ground, unmoving, listening to the rustling of the jungle. The firing ceased. The mosquitoes and leeches, lured by our fresh blood, were sheer torture.

Presently it began to rain again. The screaming con-tinued, shrill and long-drawn-out, horrible as the cry of a tortured animal. Some mortar shells fell at random, bursting against the tops of the trees, then their noise died down. At dawn nothing could be heard but a dis-mal groaning, punctuated by gasps of agony, and the monotonous patter of the rain on the leaves.

"Oh, shut that fellow up," I said.

"Watch out, that's just what they're waiting for, so as to have a pot shot at us," Conklin replied.

The Comanches undertook to clear the outskirts of the camp of the Kamikazes who were on the lookout for us.

"Leave it to them, you'll see," Learoyd had said.

It was a brilliant demonstration. We saw nothing, of

course; nor did we hear anything. At intervals shadows flitted by, as silently as the clouds. Sometimes a single shot rang out, less frequently two in succession; sometimes there was a savage screech, cut short by a sound like meat being chopped on a block.

By nine o'clock it was all over: seven rifles, stamped with the sacred emblem of the Imperial Chrysanthemum, were stacked outside the radio hut, and the flies were beginning to buzz.

Conklin was furious. He could not understand how a Japanese patrol had managed to advance this far unscathed. He tried to interrogate the wounded man, who was taking an unconscionable time to die, but it was impossible to get anything out of that hunk of gasping flesh. He then decided to finish him off and reached awkwardly for his Colt 45. The wounded man no doubt guessed the import of this gesture, for he twitched instinctively. The Colt was not cocked; the hammer struck the firing pin with a ludicrous click. The wounded man uttered a fearful hoarse cry; the will to live, the cruel will to live, was still so strong in him that he managed to twist around and stretch out his hands.

Conklin looked him straight in the eye for a moment. Something in the man's gaze must have forced him to glance away. He put his Colt back in its holster and returned to us without a word. The wounded man stayed still. We heard him gasping for some time; then we forgot all about him, and no one knew exactly when he died.

A series of explosions in the east cheered Conklin up a bit.

"The traps are working all right. Did you hear that? They're working all right now. I don't understand," he said at each fresh explosion.

On examining the aerial photographs of the region, I spotted two clearings from which the mortars might have been fired. I asked Tarakan by radio to send in the Beaufighters and bomb the approaches to them, while we struck camp and withdrew a few miles to the west. The sweetish smell of the corpses overlay the dankness imprisoned under the trees.

I spent two more days with Conklin, during which we discovered how the Japanese had managed to take us by surprise. One of their patrols going upriver by night on the last of their pirogues had landed in our rear. While scouring the forest they had run into our sentries, but the skirmish that ensued had not been to their advantage, and the survivors had been blown to pieces on booby traps as they retreated eastward. The Comanches brought us back a further half-dozen heads in an advanced state of decomposition; these Learoyd ordered to be buried so as not to attract the flies.

Fresh militias arrived; Learoyd made plans for a big raid on the Japanese flanks in conjunction with Tamong Miri's people, who hunted elephant and rhinoceros in this area. Several little groups were sent down south in search of the missing column. It was time for me to get back to my command post. I crossed the Sembakung, met Eastward on the other side, and borrowed one of the horses of the Pony Express.

The sun was just rising on the first day when I

reached the foothills of the great range overlooking the
Plain of Elephants. The land of the winds! The air
quivered, throbbed, pulsated with life.

I left my horse at the staging post and set off with
my guide up the steep slope leading to the mountain
track. As we climbed, the air grew cooler, the ranks of
forest trees more stately. The rays of sunlight piercing
through the leaves stabbed into corners of mysterious
shade, sometimes disclosing a surprising ballet of white
butterflies. Late in the afternoon we reached Viper's
Head Peak, a bare triangular basalt entablature overlooking the central basin of the Sembakung. I breathed
deeply, assailed by an inexplicable emotion. I felt free,
as free as the wind. At my feet stretched the accursed
plain, a lifeless misty ocean which merged on the horizon with the murky sky. All the Japanese armies might
have foundered in it, and no one would have known
anything about it.

I lingered there, unable to make up my mind to
leave, lying on my back, utterly happy, basking in the
sun and dreaming as I watched the clouds float by. I
suddenly felt that I understood Learoyd's aspirations,
and I was filled with compassion. To live, that was all
the poor wretch wanted—to live. To live with the de-
mands of that insatiable beast which we all have lurking
in the depths of our souls, that beast which my father
had tried to drown in drink. To live a life other than
the life of the world, to leave behind a trace of immor-
tality. Pride! . . . Man is a God-ridden animal.

Poor Learoyd, where is your victory now? King of

[163]

the wind and rain, you left behind you in that country no trace deeper than your own footprints.

It took me two more days to reach Tamong Miri via the mountain track: the Rattan Pass, the Leopard Pass, the Peak of the Spirits, the Pass of Clouds, and the Valley of the Banana Trees.

The Japanese withdrawal which had started at Tarakan was now spreading throughout Borneo. Everywhere, in the east, south, and west, the Japanese garrisons were abandoning the coastal towns to escape the Allied bombing and were moving into the jungle. Their lines of retreat appeared to converge on an assembly point as yet unknown to us, which could not be very far from the western frontier of Learoyd's kingdom.

Armstrong was worried. He was afraid we might have transferred our forces and our command post to the east too hastily. The sinister and majestic isolation of Tamong Miri in its amphitheater of forests, the black fathomless abysses of the River Srai, the monstrous banyans, the evening mist, aggravated his forebodings.

I decided to go to Senghir and see how things were working out over there. Anderson, who was bored at our new radio station up on Falcon Peak, asked to come with me. It was a tempting idea. We had just received some small American Signal Corps radios with frequency modulation which were very effective over medium distances and would enable me to keep in permanent touch with my command post.

We set off at dawn on June 4 in a London-type fog which condensed on our faces in an icy sweat. It was a delightful trip. Anderson was a perfect traveling companion, tactful, practical, tireless, and always in a good humor.

Senghir, huddled in a red blanket, perching on the ruins of his longhouse which he refused to leave, surrounded by his womenfolk—mute, sullen mummies—spent his days meditating and gazing at the vegetation running wild over his untilled rice fields. I did not get much out of him; he was singularly haughty and withdrawn:

"We have entered upon the period of fear. The southwesterly wind brings death. It's the wind of the flies. The monkeys will cry out, begging for mercy. It's a bad time, but it will come to an end, providing we live through it. Everything that is born one day must die one day—that is the law. But when the northeasterly monsoon returns, the Three Forests will still be here." He muttered in snatches punctuated by long silences.

I did not have Learoyd's patience, and these generalizations, these commonplace remarks, irritated me. I might easily have dismissed the old idiot with his goldcrammed mouth, if his cruel black birdlike eyes had not belied this hodgepodge of senile wisdom. Time went by; evening had slowly crept up on us. In the end I realized that the only thing that interested Senghir was whether Learoyd would still be King of the Muruts when the war came to an end or whether the British . . .

"Tamong Miri the Terrible is dead," he croaked. "Gwai? Bah! Gwai is still as inexperienced as a young

[166]

buffalo. It will need much wisdom to allay the madness of the young warriors."

The old scoundrel was intriguing to become Learoyd's successor. This kingdom of isolated jungle which had no legal existence was giving rise to dreams, ambitions, rivalry—even enmity perhaps.

My reply was noncommital: first of all we had to get rid of the Japanese; who could tell what would happen afterward?

That night I went to bed in the new longhouse concealed in the jungle. There I came across the young widow Learoyd had offered me as a wife and whom I had refused: a charming creature actually, with breasts like two little bronze apples and an expression full of modesty. Anderson subsequently told me she had the reputation of being a merry widow. He had been informed of this by his pal Truu Big-Belly-Button.

Next morning, June 11, Tamong Miri relayed the news of the Australian landing at Labuan, the island in the Bay of Brunei. The operation, under the code name of Oboe Six, had been directed the night before by MacArthur in person. After a fantastic bombardment by the American Seventh Fleet, 23,000 men of the 9th Australian Division had landed without any losses on the beaches near Victoria Harbor.

This was no surprise, we knew the landing was due to take place at any moment, but we were immensely cheered by the successful outcome.

On the 17th an Auster of the RAAF came to pick me up on our landing strip.

Victoria Harbor had been completely flattened by the bombardment of the fleet; only a few walls of the Rest House and a sort of ruined belfry were still standing. Bulldozers were at work carving paths through this chaos, raising clouds of heavy red dust which shimmered in the sun. The heat was stifling, the air smelled of death, and there was nothing to drink.

The artillery thundered continually. Every night stray dogs howled like wolves, and Japanese commandos launched suicide attacks. A horrible spot! Luckily Special Forces Advanced Base was installed on a magnificent beach near Collier Head. Fergusson was not there. I spent a few hours on my own, swimming, and sending big flat shells skimming over the barely rippling water. I basked stark naked on the pale sand, steeped in the savage smell of iodine and salt, gorged with heat, glutted, bludgeoned by the sun. The fiery sky absorbed the colors. I gradually allowed my mind to wander carelessly over the white desert, conscious of the muffled gong of the blood resounding in my ears.

Toward evening, though aching in every limb, burning with fever, and empty-headed, I nevertheless had to scribble a report on our activities, because Fergusson wanted to introduce me to the GOC that very night. There was no mention of Learoyd until the following morning.

"How's that Irishman of yours?" he asked me.

"When I left him, he was planning a raid against the Japanese in the east."

"Did you talk to him about . . . about his kingdom? About what's going to happen after the war?"

"Yes."

"Really? What did he say?"

"He laughed," I replied with a smile.

"He laughed, did he?"

The end of the sentence was drowned by the thunder of gunfire from a nearby battery of artillery. In the center of the island the fighting was flaring up again; during the pauses in the barrage one could hear the distant rattle of machine guns.

"I'm not sure you have a very clear idea of the simplicity and pride of the fellow," I said. "Did you know he has driven God from his kingdom?"

I told him about the missionaries. Fergusson carefully lit a cigar while listening to me, and his keen gaze disappeared behind a screen of blue smoke. When I had finished my story, he did not sneer as I had expected; he uncrossed his long legs and rose to his feet with surprising agility. He must certainly have been over fifty, but only his weary eyes betrayed his age; his body was as straight and slim as a young man's.

"Poor devil," he growled, "poor devil. Before the return of the monsoon we shall have finished off the Japanese. Then his kingdom will break up."

He took a few steps, then turned to face me and exclaimed suddenly, "And what are you up to?"

"Me?"

"Don't play the innocent. You think it's very funny, don't you? You want to see how far he'll go. Besides, he's your friend. A fine excuse for doing nothing. Well, I can tell you how all this is going to end—badly! And I can tell you what you'll do then, you'll sit on the ground

[169]

and avert your eyes. And the cock will crow thrice. It will go on crowing for the rest of your days!"

Night has fallen. I have been writing all day, and now night has fallen.

It has stopped raining. It's cold. A smoky, vaguely luminous mist is rising from the humming streets into a leaden sky reflecting the red glow from the city. The engines are hooting. This is the rush hour for suburban trains, the opening time for pubs and cinemas, the start of the working day for whores on the beat.

This is the time of day when the fettered Negroes used to be brought up from the 'tween-decks of the slave ships and made to dance and sing their hymns to life. And while they danced and sang to the moon, they forgot they were slaves and no longer dreamed of breaking their fetters.

This is the time of day when my father, abandoning the struggle, suddenly capitulated. He stretched out his hand to the big Bible on the shelf in his study and picked up the bottle of gin hidden behind it. He no longer asked his God for restlessness and glory; he begged for tranquility, stupefaction, peace of mind.

Night has fallen, I am weary with vexation of spirit.

I can still see Learoyd, a ridiculous naked little vagabond singing his hymn all alone in the forest. I can still discern him through a bank of gray mist. Soon I shall see him no longer. Farewell, noble king!

Life is a solitary accomplishment. Generation after generation, toiling to earn their daily bread, tread out their paths under the indifferent sky. They rub shoulders, they laugh and cry, they talk a great deal but understand one another little. They remain enigmas to each other. One day the father leaves his son, the friend his fellow. Farewell! Joy, whether of sage or madman, despair, whether of king or slave, terror, every sort of terror, enter into us and vex our spirits and vanish away. We are not their masters; we can only bow before them. "And all is vanity and vexation of spirit."

I am tired, I have spent the day in pursuit of the shadow of the red man with the gray eyes, who was king and who drove out God.

Cheng, clever Dr. Cheng (or Chang) used to say that Learoyd did not exist. He used to call his kingdom "the Kingdom of the Ten Thousand Illusions." But he did not like the jungle, he was a townsman. Cheng used to say, "He's a madman. He's a solitary, and men on their own have no substance, the wind blows them away. Nothing that's happening in this horrible forest has any importance."

It was true. One-half of the world was still under the sway of the spirits of evil; millions of men were massacring one another amid sound and fury. And this was only a beginning, the opening movement of a cruel symphony: this half of the world was not going to recover its balance for some time to come.

Fergusson called Learoyd a scorpion, that morning on the beach at Collier Head. A light breeze sent dark blue ripples over the sea, I remember, and the artillery was shattering our eardrums. A handful of desperate Japanese were fighting back fiercely against the Australians somewhere up in the hills. There were far more killed and wounded than those I saw brought back that evening from the regions of blood and darkness reeking of battle.

Fergusson said, "You're going to go on using him, and once the war is over, we'll make him toe the line. He'll jolly well have to toe the line! Only it's likely to kill him. Like a scorpion. You know what they do, don't you? When they feel they're done for, they sting themselves in order to die. No, it's true, you're a botanist, I believe, not a naturalist. But everyone knows that. A scorpion!"

It was true. Learoyd did toe the line. We stripped him of his glory; we tore the crown from his head; we broke him utterly, and he went off . . . he disappeared like a cloud. The Japanese colonel with the impossible name was hanged. On his last night he sent for me and told me the whole story. In the gray dawn he drank a small glass of whiskey, refused a last cigarette, and saluted ceremoniously, bowing to the ground.

"Please tell the King . . ."

And he marched out into the chill of the morning. The mist was lifting . . .

Less than a year later Fergusson killed himself, like a scorpion. Senghir became the headman of the Tribes of the West. He moved into a hideous concrete house at Tomani.

He's dead now, too. His warriors are coolies on the Sapong Estate plantation; on Saturday nights, pay day, they get roaring drunk.

"I don't know how all this is going to end, but at least I've had a good laugh."

I did not dare tell Fergusson, but that had been Learoyd's reply when I spoke to him about the future of his kingdom.

It was true. He had a good laugh, we all had a good laugh . . .

Farewell, noble king. I am weary with vexation of spirit.

This morning, on rereading these pages which I wrote yesterday at nightfall, I was on the point of tearing them up. I find them sentimental, confused, maudlin, and as usual, much more concerned with myself than with Learoyd. I have decided to keep them, however. After all, the embers I am stirring, the man I am evoking, is so distant, so dead in time and space, that if I stopped recording what I dream about him, he would cease to exist.

The night is dangerous. It disturbs the mind. In the morning life is simple. Everything falls into place in the wan light of an English winter dawn. The shadows and phantoms evaporate like a spring mist, leaving nothing but the dazzling sun, the green line of palm trees, the turquoise depths of the sea, and the sound of gunfire.

I spent several days at Labuan, trying to solve a few problems of a military nature which are not worth mentioning in detail here. It should not be thought that our main preoccupation, Fergusson's and mine, was Learoyd. Far from it. We were extremely concerned about communications between the guerrillas and the regular army. The Australians in pursuit of the Japanese were likely in their enthusiasm to regard any yellow-skinned troops as the enemy. We had to help them separate the wheat from the chaff, as it were, if we did not wish to see our Comanches massacred.

On June 19 we landed at Weston, in the estuary of the River Padas. I went in with the third assault wave. A scarlet sun was rising slowly behind a dark barrier of mangroves. For a brief moment the landing craft seemed to be sailing up a river of blood. The Navy was firing on the railway line ahead of us and the big shells went clattering over our heads like steam engines passing over a metal bridge, before bursting with an earsplitting explosion which echoed round the foothills of the Crocker Range. The earth quaked. The dust-laden air was disturbed by sudden gusts of whirling wind which smelled of gunpowder and hot steel. War. This was the real thing!

Before midday I was in contact with my radio team which, from the heights, was guiding the attacks of the fighter-bombers in support. That evening a roving Australian patrol ran into the defense group without firing on it. This was a success.

Next morning the Australians resumed their advance along the railway line toward Beaufort. There was some fierce fighting. (It was in this sector, I believe, that the last Victoria Cross of the war was awarded, to a private soldier.*) The collaboration between my militias

* Private T. Starcevitch, from Kalgoorlie.

[175]

and the army proved effective, and there were no untoward incidents. I went back to Labuan.

On the 21st I touched down on our landing strip in the interior. The valley was peaceful and silent, the air smelled fresh, the earth rich. Corbett, with the help of Dr. Cheng (or Chang), had opened the hospital. The young missionary had died; his tomb, marked with a cross, was near the torrent on a little hill which served as our graveyard. His companion, the old priest with the granite face, was trotting merrily to and fro between our first battle casualties and our civilian patients. He was not at all embarrassed by the naked breasts of the village girls, and every morning, on waking, he would exclaim, "How beautiful is God's creation! Long live Our Lord!"

He prayed on his knees for the dying, but he took care not to engage in proselytism. Everyone liked him. Yoo and her son had joined Learoyd in Tamong Miri. Anderson was teaching again in the school. He also made a number of kites for the children to play with.

I had arranged a rendezvous with Armstrong to see how things stood. The military situation had clarified since my departure. We now knew the spot on which the Japanese armies were converging: the rubber plantation of the Sapong Estate, north of Tomani on the River Padas. It was a judicious choice. The only means of access for the Australians who had landed on the coast was the cleft made by the river, a magnificent gorge fifteen miles long through which the railway line barely squeezed, a deep gash right through the Crocker Range, a death trap in which many were to die.

The three hazards menacing Learoyd's kingdom

were less serious than we had at first thought. In the west the Japanese columns, harassed by the Dayaks of Sarawak, would skirt the frontier through the territory of the Red Dogs and Tomani. In the south they would have vast uninhabited areas to cross; they would not be arriving for some time. There remained the east. Here lay the real danger: to reach the Sapong Estate, the army from Tarakan would have to cross the kingdom from one side to the other.

I left Armstrong in command of the western front. He did extremely well and won the DSO. Relying on Senghir's authority, he coordinated all the guerrilla actions and even succeeded in infiltrating into the plantation some radio teams who guided the attacks of the bombers. (It was about this time that we made the villagers of Tomani kill their dogs so that their barking should not give away our movements to the enemy. Only one animal escaped; he fled into the jungle and for several months, long after the war had ended, he used to howl all night in the eerie silence of the valley.)

I reached Tamong Miri after a three days' forced march, guided by one of the runners of the Pony Express. It was raining, of course. The amphitheater of forest, engulfed in thick clouds, seemed more sinister than ever, and the longhouse, which was completely silent, gave me the same dismal impression of abandonment as the old dismantled schooners which sometimes, when I was a child, used to serve as shelters for the harbor tramps in winter.

There were two half-naked witches chewing betel near a fire of glowing embers. At the far end of the room

[177]

a feeble torch pierced the darkness, shedding a flickering light on three recumbent figures. That was all, there was nothing else. I was at the end of the world, and the last men appeared to have fled, as though at the approach of some apocalyptic cataclysm, leaving behind them only a couple of scarecrows. Outside, the light was fading fast. The rain pelted down relentlessly. The water was going to rise slowly, steadily, like a silent tide, gradually engulfing the forest, the entire valley. Or else, with a tremendous roar, the undermined mountains would collapse into rivers of mud and all trace of life would be wiped from the face of the earth.

A dog sniffed at me, growling and baring its teeth. I was shivering with cold in my drenched combat jacket. The more decrepit of the two witches spat out her quid of betel and jabbered something I could not understand. A human form stirred at the end of the room, and I recognized Yoo. Learoyd was lying beside her under a blanket which clung to his cadaverous frame like a shroud. His teeth were chattering and he exuded almost as much heat as the glowing embers. Only half his face was visible in the light. He peered at me for a moment with a glassy eye.

With an effort, he mumbled something incomprehensible.

His voice sounded strange. His mouth remained hanging open. He had no strength left to close it. His unseeing eyes returned to the mysterious contemplation of some distant object beneath the shadows of the roof.

Conklin was asleep, curled up under a parachute. I

drew closer and called to him, but he did not budge. His forehead was burning; he, too, looked terribly emaciated.

"Sick. Very sick," Yoo muttered.

The flame of the torch was reflected in her black moist eyes, so eloquent in distress. I tried to extract some details but quickly gave up; her English was too faltering and I was too tired. It was easy to guess what had happened. Fever, microbes, the viruses lurking in the air and the mud of the Plain of Elephants had finally taken their toll. It was more difficult to understand why the longhouse had been abandoned like this; did the Muruts believe this fever was contagious?

In their corner the two fateful witches started squawking shrilly. They were a horrible sight, both of them, bent, dirty, toothless, grimacing in the glow of the embers, but the row they made was even worse. I don't know what they were trying to say; to me it sounded like some dreadful portent. Poor old hags, clinging to life!

Yoo silenced them in a curt voice. They whimpered a bit, then at last calmed down.

My eyelids were drooping with fatigue. I undressed, curled up under a parachute, and fell asleep at once.

At dawn the overcast sky looked even more sinister than the night before. There was a brief, blood-red sunrise, then the mass of clouds closed in again and the light turned ashen.

I was awakened by cries of merriment. The little potbellied prince was playing with his father. Yoo was still asleep. The two old witches lay huddled under some blankets by the dying fire.

Learoyd was laughing, but his emaciation and weakness transformed his laughter into an unendurable grimace; he looked like a grinning skeleton. Conklin was munching the contents of a tin of corned beef. Their fever had gone.

Four days earlier they had left the heights, feeling ill, and had dragged themselves down here. Cheng (or Chang) had treated them by radio. They were afraid they might have caught cholera or something worse, but it was only pernicious malaria, and massive doses of quinine had almost killed them.

Conklin gave me his report:

"The Japs appeared on Viper's Head. They crowded together up there to enjoy a little sunshine and breathe some fresh air. The air force turned up, it was sheer slaughter! You should have seen them tumbling into the valley." He chuckled, revealing long yellow teeth. "I don't think they'll climb on to the heights again in a hurry. They're at the Rattan Pass now, but they haven't got across it. Eastward, Bren, and Gwai are seeing to that."

This effort had exhausted him. He sank back on the rolled-up parachutes and closed his eyes, but went on talking in a low voice.

"They're suffering, more than we are. A lot of them are sick—they just abandon them on the track. Some of them have hanged themselves with their belts. They're short of grub. They've got hardly any heavy arms left."

"Good show, old boy. Now I'm going to have you transported to our hospital, you need proper treatment."

"No, sir. No, I'm all right. The fever lasted three days. The Chink told us it would. It's over now, I'll get better."

He begged me to leave him at Tamong Miri and not to send him to the west. I could well understand him. I, too, was fascinated by this sinister spot and had no intention of leaving before everything was finished.

"You know, I've brought off some lovely 'breaks,' " he concluded weakly.

The little gray-eyed prince was still chortling with joy. He kept toddling up, belly thrust forward, flinging himself on his father, roaring with laughter, constantly interrupting the Pony Express runner who had guided me there the previous evening. Each time this happened, Learoyd laughed, hugged the child, rubbed him against his unshaven chin, then went on talking to the runner. His face was ravaged, his eyes betrayed intense fatigue, but he looked happy.

He raised himself on one elbow, and called to me, "Well, did you hatch your plot with the old crow? It seems he wants to take over from me after the war."

Only the women had been present at my conversation with Senghir. In surprise I replied, "How did you know?"

"Governing means knowing. I know everything."

"No doubt it's my widow, the merry widow . . ."

He interrupted me with a derisive laugh, "So they told you she was merry, did they? Now that you've seen her, you must be sorry you said no, eh?" Then, resuming his serious tone, he went on, "He is old and wise. That's to say weary and disillusioned. Don't count on him if you want to get the better of me."

"But I've no intention of getting the better of you," I said.

His gray eyes, deep and unfathomable as the sea, looked at me a long time.

"Not now. Later. I'm telling you before it happens."

At midday Conklin connected the American S.C.R. 300 and got through to Eastward on the Rattan Pass. The Japanese had taken advantage of the bad weather, which kept the air force grounded, to try a forced passage, but Bren's machine guns and mortars had halted them again. Eastward said their wounded could be heard screaming in the mist.

"They were camouflaged with branches, and at dawn I thought the whole wood began to move," I heard him say through the crackling of the receiver.

The rain came down again. A thin mist steamed from the saturated earth. The black rock of Falcon Peak and the grim amphitheater of forest disappeared—obliterated, dissolved, submerged, liquefied. Everything seemed intermingled, as on the morning of the second day of the creation, and no one could have said for certain where water, sky, or land began.

At dusk the dog barked. A horde of glistening warriors burst in. An outbreak of shouts and laughter, a torrent of life, hirsute and savage, invaded the longhouse. Big fires were lit; the flames flickered on bronze

[182]

skins glittering with raindrops, gleamed on the well-oiled steel of weapons. They squatted in a circle around their king. Dragon jars were brought in. They drank the ayak in great gulps.

There were men there from every tribe in the kingdom, from the Red Lands, the Black Lands, the Upper Sembakung and its tributaries, the northern borders, the Plain of Elephants. They had come down from the heights. They had marched for two days, carrying their wounded. They had come to fetch more shells for the mortars and ammunition belts for the machine guns.

The three wounded men, lying mute under some Australian Army ponchos, were brought to Learoyd so that he might see and touch them—one of them was already stamped with the mark of death—then they were carried close to a fire and entrusted to the care of the two old crones. The little gray-eyed prince observed them intently for some time.

The famished warriors ate and drank; the sound of champing jaws and the murmur of voices were punctuated every now and then by a rasping laugh like the cry of a jackal. They described their battles and imitated the discomfiture of their enemies. As their drunkenness increased, so did the animal scent of their sweat. Those who were slightly wounded tore off their dressings to allow the blood to flow and to enable Learoyd to admire their courage and know what part they had played in the fighting, for a lie may be believed, but what the eye beholds is truth.

Yoo reigned over this barbaric feast with her beauty,

[183]

the firmness of her breasts, the velvet texture of her belly, and the glory of her thighs. The flames cast rust-colored reflections on her bare amber skin. All the warriors were eyeing her. She was resplendent.

Many hours later the last drunken warrior staggered to his feet, breathing heavily, weaved his way among the recumbent forms of his comrades, and collapsed in a corner like a lifeless hulk.

Then there was nothing but silence. Silence and the monotonous gurgle of the rain.

Then the wounded men felt lonely, and the darkness beyond the glowing embers fading into sparks filled them with fear. They groaned, and the one who was to die uttered a strange cry three times, like a call for help.

I think I was the only one who heard him. I could have gone over and held his hand. I don't know why I remained lying on my back, with my eyes wide open and a painful sensation of distress clawing at my heart.

Sometimes, even today, I recall that cry in the night.

In the morning he was dead. Yoo and the two old witches set out the offerings—a handful of rice, a handful of meat, half a dozen rounds of ammunition, and some calao quills—chanting a plaintive dirge and brushing away the flies that were beginning to buzz. The men of his tribe went off to dig a grave in the forest. He was buried standing upright, with his head-hunter's sword.

I had decided to climb up to the heights with the

ammunition convoy. I said goodbye to Learoyd and Conklin. Their temperatures were back to normal, but they both needed a few days' convalescence to recover their strength before joining me.

Learoyd told me the name of the dead warrior and the name of his village, but I have forgotten them.

The Battle of the Heights (as we subsequently called it
among ourselves) lasted almost a month and culminated
in a night of horror, one of those when men go raving
mad. It was actually a succession of battles at the passes:
the Rattan Pass, the Leopard Pass, the Pass of Clouds,
the Pass of Monkeys. Each of these engagements was
blood-drenched, and on some days gusts of feverish wind
wafted the stench of death and the abominable buzzing
of the flies right up to us.

On several occasions, in the chill of dawn, in the
rain, through the fog, I saw the silent wood begin to
move. At night we sometimes heard strange cries, like
wild animals answering one another, when the Japanese
were preparing for an attack; we would then light big
fires on the hilltops to enable our aircraft to take their
bearings despite the darkness.

Our purpose was not to halt the Japanese; we didn't
have enough men or arms for that. Our purpose was to
deny them access to the fertile valleys, to force them to
deflect their lines of withdrawal toward the uninhabited
north by way of the unhealthy reaches of the tributaries

of the Lower Sembakung. We were almost successful. Unfortunately communications between our Comanche units were continually hampered because we found no one able to read. When the phantom column which had disappeared south of the Plain of Elephants emerged in our rear, an order was inaccurately interpreted, and the Pass of Clouds remained open for the whole of one night.

But before describing this disaster, I must pick up the thread of events.

After a short time Learoyd and Conklin joined me. They were still in poor condition, and it took them hours to climb the last slopes. After every step they would stop, their eyes glazed, panting for breath. The muscles of the lean legs quivered visibly. Learoyd kept repeating the words of his captain who had been killed on the River Slim during the withdrawal from Malaya: "If I think you're alive, I think of you marching."

He was like a skeleton marching, but he had such vital force that he recovered astonishingly quickly. Conklin took a little longer, but the prospect of rejoining his desert rats and resuming his dynamiting activities, plus a few tins of corned beef, eventually restored him completely.

Eastward died.

It was an accident. Some Comanches were fiddling with a Japanese weapon they had taken from a corpse to see how it worked. The weapon was booby-trapped. The explosive bullet struck Eastward in the nape of the neck. When Learoyd and I arrived, he was lying on his back, his huge, scarlet, shattered face turned toward the

[187]

sun. It was impossible for us to close his eyes. Hundreds of flies rose, buzzing furiously, from the pool of blood and brains on the ground.

Later on I was to see something even more frightful. While making my way up the sandbanks of the Tabuk Libang (Learoyd's gold river), which had been the scene of fierce fighting, I noticed the black form of a recumbent man. As I drew level with it, the form suddenly disappeared in a cloud of flies. There was nothing left, nothing. Only the flies and the stench of death. My foot sank into something foul and mushy. Lying there, invisible under a thin layer of gold-bearing sand, was the body of a Japanese; after I had moved on, the black, quivering, rustling form of this vanished soldier instantly resumed shape. I marched for a long time in the river to wash my boots clean.

The Comanches of Eastward's militia sat squatting on their haunches, silent and grim. One of them came up to Learoyd and spoke to him.

"What did he say?" I asked.

"He's the headman," Learoyd replied. "He said, 'Many of the warriors are still bad men; like blades one would have keen, they cut the man sharpening them.' He said, 'My tribe is ready to pay the blood money.' That means they will give you as many dragon jars as it is fitting to demand for the life of a man."

"And what did you say to that?" I asked.

"I told him there were not enough dragon jars on this earth to redeem the blood of all the men who are going to die. I also told him—oh, our sort of thing, poetry, as you call it."

[188]

Eastward was buried on the Peak of the Spirits, standing upright like a Murut warrior. He had enough offerings to make a long voyage into the beyond. I had refused to let his carbine be buried with him, and the headman slipped into his hands his own head-hunter's sword with the rhinoceros-horn hilt. The grave was marked with a cross, and I recited the funeral service that my father had made me learn by heart because he considered it worth meditating upon: "Man that is born of woman hath but a short time to live . . ."

On their slow migration the Japanese were never able to light a fire: by day smoke rising through the vault of the trees is visible from the air or from any surrounding height; by night a flame can be seen in spite of the density of the jungle; by day and night the Comanches can detect the smell of burning wood a long way off. We could not light fires either when we were on the hunt. We slept huddled together to try to conserve a little heat; we munched cold rice which had the sour taste of bile.

The rain and the sun made us ferment. The tall grass brushed our faces like clammy hands with icy fingers. The wild beasts fled; we caught the scent of fear. We had enough imagination and youthfulness in those days to accept the knowledge that at any moment everything might come to an end here, in a pool of warm blood. We lived for the present, in a space limited to a few yards' visibility, and when the hazards of our deadly quest led us through a clearing in the forest, we stood

[189]

dazzled, our noses in the air, to gape at clouds drifting past.

The Battle of Leopard Pass was a great victory. For the first time we took a lot of prisoners. In the evening the Japanese beat a retreat. Their bugle calls sounded like sobs in the darkness of the valley.

Next day Learoyd sent me a message asking me to join him in a longhouse a few hours' march away. I arrived at nightfall. A score of prisoners, emaciated and in tattered uniforms, were smartly drawn up on either side of the track, waving torches. The dogs kept barking, and the assembled villagers lashed out at them indignantly.

Learoyd was waiting for me, standing at the top of the veranda steps. The old Comanche guard were milling about behind him, already a little the worse for ayak. A little Jap with a sickly expression was desperately blowing a sort of clarinet (a *shakuhachi*). The somewhat melancholy but lovely music could scarcely be heard above the uproar.

As soon as he saw me Learoyd yelled delightedly: "Banzai!"

It was an incredible bash, and the wretched trembling musician was forced to play all night for our entertainment. Among the prisoners were two women, two nurses who had been captured with a field hospital. At the end of the meal, which they served us on their knees in the Japanese manner, Learoyd declared with a dignified air, "We are victorious and you are my guest. You can choose whichever you like, and I'll have the other."

His eyes, sparkling with pleasure, watched me

[190]

closely. Since I remained speechless, he added, "I made them have a bath. They're quite clean."

The two women were still on their knees in front of us. Their impassive Asiatic faces were devoid of expression. They were lovely, at least I thought them so, though rather thin.

"Oh, they're quite happy, you know. They were convinced we were going to cut off their heads. The little one even tried to poison herself," Learoyd went on.

I spent the night with the taller of the two. She had skin as fresh and smooth as ivory and a pathetic little body like an immature schoolgirl's, marked by the two pink tips of her breasts and the small cleft mound of her sex. She shut her eyes and uncrossed her legs, but did not move. She remained inert. Her face was a mask.

I didn't mind. What were her hostility or disgust, what was her soul to me? I wanted to take, use, and cast aside. I wanted my pleasure, rapid and brutal, I wanted to feel the pulsing of my blood; what was another's life to me? After all, tomorrow I would climb back to those bloody mountain peaks, bury myself once more in that sinister valley without fires or laws, and perhaps a bullet . . . Then all this would have existed only in the brain of Uncle Bôo, the diabolical little mouse-deer who calls the tune.

Once, however, I felt her quiver, her lips parted; she tried to bite them to control herself, but was unable to withstand the mounting surge. Her arms tightened behind my neck, and for an instant I saw in her eyes how much of flesh there is in the spirit.

I woke up in the morning as brisk as a young animal,

[191]

with a sense of well-being devoid of remorse. My impassive Japanese girl avoided my eyes; to show my affection, I gave her a gentle tap on the behind.

While Learoyd ravenously tucked in to a breakfast of grasshoppers and wild honey, his little nurse manifested the most enchanting gratitude toward him. There was not an ounce of vice or immodesty in their frolics; they were both utterly immoral and charming. The wretched musician was again blowing his *shakuhachi* in a corner. He looked even more sickly and pitiful than the evening before, and he played much less well. I fancied he cast an angry glance in my direction.

"I like his music, it's a change from the Comanche army marching songs, but the blighter won't play anything more cheerful," Learoyd said good-humoredly. Then he added, with all the casualness in the world: "Did you know your girl is married? I rather think he's the husband."

This idea put him in such high spirits that he almost choked with laughter. I found his joke neither funny nor decent, and I told him so.

"I didn't know anything about it last night, honest," he replied, "and we're not going to cry over that, are we?"

True, we were not going to cry over that.

"Make him stop, his music depresses me."

The blighter almost got me into serious trouble after the war. In the internment camp on the Sapong Estate he told the Red Cross that I had raped his wife. The British Army does not care for that sort of thing.

[192]

Luckily he died in the hospital before the court of inquiry was held.

Rain, mist, sun, the wind on the heights. Human footprints, the rattle of bullets, the linked explosions of Dynamite Dave's booby traps. Sour rice . . .

The days went by.

The Japanese drifted slowly northward.

I saw my first hanged man. I heard him before seeing him because of the flies. He had chosen as his gallows the low branch of a huge banyan wreathed in parasitical plants. He looked like some poisonous fruit.

Fergusson touched down on our landing strip but did not push on to Tamong Miri. He stayed in the west and conferred with Armstrong and Senghir. I was able to speak to him, however, thanks to our little FM radios. Learoyd refused to leave the front to meet him.

"I know what he's going to say. And I'm not interested."

Rain, mist, sun . . .

In the accursed depths of the valleys the Japanese corpses, daily increasing in number, were so skeleton-thin that they hardly stank at all. In a short while the ants and worms had picked them clean. The sick who had been abandoned, the stragglers, buried their useless rifles, slithered like snakes into the thick undergrowth, and lay down on their hand grenades after first removing the pin. We found one body with a thigh missing. It had not been blown off by an explosion. It had been

[193]

neatly amputated at hip level by a surgeon—or by a butcher. During the next few days we came across others.

In the evening we could hear the groans of the dying, death rattles, shrieks of raving terror. My God, how long men take to die!

Rain, mist . . .

On July 15 the phantom column was spotted three days' march away, southwest of Tamong Miri, on the right bank of the Sembakung. It was over two months since it had disappeared in the Plain of Elephants. According to our information, it was about a thousand strong. The men must have been well disciplined and well commanded to have given us the slip for so long.

Learoyd and I decided to dispatch Conklin and his gang of dynamiters "to prepare the ground for them," as he put it. He let off a few firecrackers all right; in fact there was a regular firework display. At last he was up against proper soldiers, no longer a screen of terrified Javanese; and they reacted like proper soldiers, as he had predicted.

At the same time the militias at Tamong Miri were transferred to the Sembakung by way of the Srai. Orders to this effect were sent by radio to Bren Lewis, who was roving somewhere up on the Pass of Monkeys. Learoyd confirmed all these decisions by runner.

A misunderstanding occurred, an order was inaccurately interpreted.

Subsequently Bren felt he was to blame. I saw him standing in front of Learoyd with tears in his eyes: "It's me, it's my fault. I should have known."

Learoyd, deathly pale, dismissed him without a word.

It was not Bren's fault. He was more than six hours' march away, alone with a horde of warriors whose language he could barely understand. He could not do everything, see everything, know everything. It was the fault of no one person. It was an accident, the wind of hazard. Fate.

On July 17 it was raining. We were blinded by the icy downpour. Like wolves, we were following the tracks of a small exhausted troop of Japanese, and we already knew that they would not escape us.

Shortly before nightfall a panting runner caught up with us and told us the news: the militia in position on the Pass of Clouds had moved down to the Sembakung. The pass lay open. The Japanese had swept through and were streaming down the Valley of the Banana Trees.

There ensued a headlong race through the night.

There ensued a headlong race through the night.

Learoyd forged ahead like an enraged buffalo, like a maddened wild boar fighting its way through the undergrowth, and we followed his trail. For three hours we skirted the course of a torrent, up to our waists in water. Despite the probable presence of the Japanese, we had to light torches of dead bamboo and resin, which blazed in the rain with big bright flames; our twisting shadows leaped behind us on the glistening foliage.

We left the torrent to head straight for the crest through a chaos of crumbling jagged limestone rocks, which we climbed with bleeding hands, our breath coming in gasps. The vegetation clung to us, damp and suffocating in its stench, enveloping us in a mantle of stickiness.

We reached the crest. It was no longer raining, but the faint breeze moaning in the branches made us shiver with cold. I could not have gone another step. Learoyd wanted to push on without stopping. This man, whom I had believed to be at death's door only three weeks before, had an incredible resilience; it was as though the jungle of his kingdom gave him a mysterious access to energy. That night, moreover, anguish and desperation drove him on: the Valley of the Banana Trees, down which the Japanese were moving from the Pass of Clouds, led straight to the Srai and Tamong Miri's longhouse. Before starting off again, however, we had to contact Bren by radio (we had been unable to do so down in the valley). I also got through to Tarakan to advise the Beaufighters to stand by.

Shortly before dawn we heard two muffled detonations.

It was already light, the livid light of a new day being born, when we reached a little hillock on the edge of the clearings around the village. It was raining slightly, not the violent rain of the tropics but an icy drizzle, a watery haze that hung in the air like an English autumn mist.

The Japanese rear guard was crossing the Srai in good order. They looked like a procession of big clumsy insects. Our machine guns pinned them down in the water, breaking the oppressive silence of the forest amphitheater with a sudden roll of thunder. The big insects scattered in fright, struggling among the bullets which pocked the water into tall white plumes. The clatter of the weapons amplified tenfold by the mountain echo, the smell of gunpowder and hot oil were intoxicating.

The Comanches fired in short, deliberate, cruel bursts. Only a handful of men succeeded in reaching the shelter of the trees on the opposite bank. They re-

[197]

turned an accurate fire that whistled spitefully past our ears.

Three Japs came running out of the longhouse. One of them was carrying a big sack. I picked him off with a shot from my carbine. He stopped dead in his tracks, took one more faltering step, then fell to his knees. He remained kneeling, hanging his head, swaying slightly, for what seemed to me an endless space of time. I had the impression I could see the life seeping out of him. Since then, in Spain, I have seen a bull killed in the arena. The sword was buried up to the hilt in its body, red bubbles oozed from its nostrils and mingled with its saliva, and it, too, swayed, glassy-eyed, obstinately trying to keep on its feet. The matador looked at it, then slowly turned away.

Suddenly the Jap toppled over on his side and lay still. The two others crumpled up, riddled by the machine gun, before ever reaching the river.

A terrifying silence descended, without one cry, one shot. The silence of death itself. Learoyd was already racing across the vegetable patches toward the house. It was quite a distance to cover, a gentle slope bristling with blackened stumps, then a ravine. I was in no hurry to follow him. I knew what he was going to find.

It was raining but the clouds were not low. I connected the radio and instructed the relay team that Bren had installed on Falcon Peak to call up the Beaufighters standing by at Tarakan.

The persistent silence was nerve-racking. I felt it to be as tenuous as the thread holding the sword of Destiny above our heads. And suddenly the thread snapped.

The forest started howling. A raucous concert, guttural cries, hisses, strident ululations like the shrilling of cicadas, sharp yelps, an uproar of confused and desperate violence: the monkeys. Every morning the monkeys wake at first light and give tongue like this, but I had never heard them so close to a village before, and never in the neighborhood of the Tamong Miri amphitheater. On the banks of the Srai the trees seemed shaken by a wild wind. The Japanese fired a few shots. A black body tumbled from branch to branch and landed with a crash in the tall grass. The cries ceased at once, but a silent storm swept the treetops all the way up to the heights and the passes; one could follow its passage like a ripple on the sea.

A Comanche raised his rifle and aimed at the spot where the black monkey had fallen. Far off, muffled by distance, the desperate cacophony started up again. I remembered what old Senghir had told me in the ruins of his longhouse: "Monkeys will cry out, begging for mercy."

The Comanche stood as motionless as a pointer. Down by the river, on the far bank, the grass rustled slightly. He fired, three times. The bullets tore through the grass and all was calm again. The Comanche lowered his rifle without ceasing to watch the bank. He muttered something in which I could make out the word "Nippon," and raised his hand to his mouth, miming the motions of eating. I understood that a starving Jap had tried to recover the body of the monkey.

Bren turned up with his mortars and machine guns just as the Beaufighters came hurtling through the

[199]

clouds. He went into the longhouse, but came out at once, green in the face, like a wounded man leaving the battlefield in order to be sick. I guided the aircraft in. They carried out a low-altitude attack on the approaches to the river (for the first time I saw the oblong containers of napalm descending, revolving on their own axes, and landing in a ball of fire and a cloud of black smoke), then they machine-gunned the jungle and the track running through a ravine toward the Great Mountain of the Dead (Golgotha, the place of the skull, as the Australian pilots nonchalantly called it, because from the air it resembled a bald head).

I doubt very much whether these attacks were particularly effective, but it was a heartening sight. We all watched in fascination as those flaming suns and clouds of darkness blotted out the sky.

The Japanese bugles sounded in the distance.* Their calls, which we could hear now and again above the roar of the aircraft, sounded like the very voice of rage, of pain, of human despair.

It was raining. It was cold. Oh, how cold it was! The rain streamed down our faces like tears.

Tamong Miri's longhouse was a tomb, dark, fetid, and buzzing. I was assailed by a charnel-house stench mingled with the suffocating reek of burned flesh. Large green flies settled on my face, fanning the air with their wings. One of the wretched witches had toppled over

---

* Since the Japanese had no more wireless transmitters in working order, this was their only means of communication; they had to remain in close formation in order to survive.

into the fire and the glowing embers were consuming her face. There was a shapeless form lying beside her, which I thought I recognized as her companion.

I looked for Yoo and found myself splashing through black liquid which clung to my boots. There were bodies everywhere, killed in various ways but all hideously mutilated. Our wounded, in transit for Cheng's hospital, had been pinned with bayonets to the bamboo partitions. Everything was smashed and ravaged. All that remained of the dog was its skin.

Yoo was nothing but a mass of red pulp raped by the barrel of a rifle. I recognized her by her hair. Blood. Blood everywhere. And the head of the little prince, his gray eyes wide open on all this blood. Only his head. We found the rest of his body, hacked to pieces, in the sack carried by the man I had shot.

The Comanches, heads bowed, wandered about in silence in the rain. They did not want to shelter in the longhouse, nor even to take cover between the piles, for the blood had run down these also. They wandered about, numbed and dismal.

Learoyd stood motionless, arms folded, glistening. I attempted to speak to him. He raised his hand and the look in his eyes stopped me in my tracks; he wanted to be left alone. I don't know what he was thinking—who could say?—I only know his eyes frightened me. They were as fathomless and inscrutable as ever, but beneath their icy surface I suspected—as one suspects the murky waters in certain chasms of concealing monstrous creatures in their depths—I suspected a somber pride and an immense, an absolute and irremediable loneliness.

[201]

Yes, his eyes frightened me at that moment and I avoided his gaze. He too, no doubt, had no wish that I should read him: he turned his back on me and walked heavily away, plunging deeper still into his solitude.

Sorrow, cold, weariness, the all-pervading stench of corruption and blood clouded my mind and precluded all decent thought. Then something horrible happened which made me burst out laughing: a scraggy man, bent double, with a bewildered expression on his face, appeared at the top of the steps of the longhouse. Dazzled by the light, he stood for an instant swaying like a drunkard, blithely muttering unintelligible words. He was a Japanese straggler who had been left behind. He must have fallen asleep in some corner and had just waked up.

We all thought he was drunk. Today I am convinced that he was mad, that he had gone mad. We had all gone mad!

Eventually he identified us; it was the transformation of his face, his surprise and consternation, that appeared so comical to me and triggered off my laughter. A host of arms brandishing swords were upraised and I saw no more of him. He was fairly—fairly, what a euphemism! —hacked to pieces.

It was raining. It was cold. I ordered big fires to be lit.

Toward midday the sun came out and blazed down on us. The air became crystal clear, the sky limpid and blue; the amphitheater of forest sparkled like a casket of emeralds of which the gem, as it were, was this stinking, buzzing longhouse.

"I'm tired," Learoyd said.

I think those were the only words in English that he uttered that day.

During the day the militias we had recalled from the Sembakung arrived. They were magnificent. They were fierce and savage, bristling with weapons. Their supple gait, their proud bearing, their resolute air had something fearsome and inspiring about them; they were a transfusion of life.

Learoyd got up, issued orders; some runners set off for the west. He made each of the new arrivals look around the longhouse, but he himself did not enter it again.

The war gongs sounded. One after another the flying squads of blowpipes crossed the Srai and plunged into the jungle on the heels of the Japanese. Bren and his mortars were the last to leave, over the Pass of Monkeys and along the heights.

In the evening, when the last rays of the orange sun gleamed on the somber outcrop of Falcon Peak, this sinister day ended with an explosion, screams of pain, bloodshed. More bloodshed! Learoyd had given orders for the bodies to be brought out of the longhouse and buried; they had been booby-trapped. Two Comanches, two good companions of the old guard, were seriously wounded. One of them died while being transported to the hospital.

During the days that followed we were merciless. We did not take a single prisoner.

At dawn we abandoned the smoking ruins of Tamong Miri's longhouse. Learoyd had set fire to it. It had blazed in the starry night like a huge red beacon.

We followed the Japanese along their Via Dolorosa. Many of them had reached the depths of despair. They were exhausted. They preferred to die. The others pushed on in close file, groping their way through the mountains, seeking to discover a way out. There was no sky for them, there was no sun for them, no stars, no hope, nothing but the dank gloom of the forest, the hunger in the belly. If I think of this trek nowadays, I think of a descent into darkness.

First of all I saw the body of the monkey in the blackened grass, then the body of the starving Jap who had tried to retrieve it. Both were roasted to a turn. A little farther on, behind the trees, the napalm had grilled three or four more soldiers of the rear guard who must have been waiting there, dribbling with greed, for their comrades to return. I think this was the total score that could be chalked up to the Air Force.

In the afternoon we came across the men who had

hanged themselves. We counted fourteen of them before the sun went down. There were other corpses on the ground, convulsed, with swollen bellies, their faces hideously contorted as if tortured. The wretches had eaten the raw paddy they had found in the longhouse. Some had ended their misery by putting a bullet through their brains.

Next day we caught up with the stragglers. First of all isolated ones, too weak to walk, whom we finished off one by one. Then small groups who fought back fiercely. A madman in a tree fired his last round at us before casting himself into the void with a rope around his neck.

From the heights Bren's mortars kept pounding the head of the Japanese column, whose horizon was blocked by the Great Mountain of the Dead. Our flying squads hovered about its flanks. We were like leeches on a strong body weakening, like red ants on a dying caterpillar. At every moment we knew exactly what the Japanese were up to, whereas they knew nothing, saw nothing, and when they heard something it was too late. We sliced the column into several sections which struggled separately, like a cut-up worm.

By the last gleams of daylight we surrounded a strong detachment. All night long the bugle called for help. Cries. Cries and more cries. "Learoyd am I!" The laughter and the sob of the head-hunters.

The Japanese concentrated their forces. They fought back. They had no wish to die. They were superb. All night long the bugle called for help, but there was no help, there was no hope. The awesome night was red with blood.

All night long Learoyd killed.

At the seventh hour of the morning, when the jungle slowly turned gray, the bulge ceased to call. Then Learoyd the King stopped and regarded his handiwork.

It was not until the next day, however, that his eyes were opened and he saw that he was naked.

The following day was August 6, 1945, the day of the bombing of Hiroshima. During the whole of the 5th we had remained near the battlefield. In the pale dawn of victory we had first to bury our dead and evacuate the wounded to Cheng's hospital.

Then we reorganized our front. Taking advantage of the self-sacrifice of their comrades and the gap left by the militias who had abandoned their positions to join in the slaughter, the Japanese columns had welded together again and succeeded in forcing the crossing of the Tabuk Libang, the River of Gold. We launched our flying squads after them.

Sobered by the silence, the Comanches, with drooping shoulders and vacant expressions, wandered about like sleepwalkers among the Japanese dead. They came upon the bugle and made a few ridiculous noises on it, which cheered them up a bit. I sat there for some time, not knowing what to do, incapable of sorting out my thoughts, filled with a tumult of sensations and memories that rose and receded like the ebb and flow of the tide.

Learoyd slept restlessly and woke up mute and morose. We hardly exchanged a word. Toward five in the afternoon we moved off because the stench and the flies were becoming unbearable.

On August 6 the weather was splendid; it had rained in the night, but the mist had cleared and the air was as fresh as on a spring morning. The hairless skull of the Mountain of the Dead, a huge black rampart, sparkled in the rising sun.

We were following an easy track leading through a little valley to the River of Gold when we saw the Japanese. There were eight of them—I remember the number exactly—eight, one more than the number of bullets in a Colt 45. All eight were lying in the middle of the track, in convulsed attitudes, and at first I thought they too had eaten raw paddy. One was curled up in a ball, like a sick child; another, flat on his stomach, was clutching his rifle, his cheek resting against the butt; a third lay spread-eagled on the ground. They were horribly emaciated and their joints looked like knotted rope. There was something strange about the silence brooding over this massacre, and I did not immediately realize its dreadful significance.

There were no flies buzzing around. These men were not dead.

They had each been struck by two or three poison-tipped arrows, in the back and thighs. They had tried to pluck them out from one another, but had snapped them off in the process. They had panicked. They had run and fallen. Some had gouged at their wounds with their knives in an attempt to remove the poisoned tips. They had started to suffer, then they had been gradu-

[207]

ally overcome by paralysis. They must have been at-
tacked two days before, or was this the group that had
slipped through our fingers during the night battle? Had
they been overtaken the next morning by our flying
squads?

At all events they had been lying here for at least
thirty-six hours, unable to move a muscle, in the sun
and the rain. The ants, the insects, the little carnivores,
attracted by the blood from their wounds, had begun to
eat them alive. They were so completely immobilized,
so utterly helpless, that they could not even pluck off
the leeches that were devouring their eyes.

What life remained was concentrated in their eyes—
the terrible will to live, in their eyes! Like an animal,
crouching, trapped. I could read nothing there but fear,
unnamable fear, frantic terror. There was nothing else.

Learoyd took out his Colt. The shot rang out like
cannon fire in the silence of the valley. I jumped as
though I had been hit myself. Learoyd had finished off
the first man and was now walking toward the second.
His footsteps echoed as loudly as the beating of my
heart. The Jap's eyes blinked as the footsteps approached him. His eyelids drooped for a moment. The
tension relaxed. There was a sort of weary acquiescence
in the depths of his eyes, a sudden melancholy calm, the
terror was less unbearable.

Seven times running the expression in the victims'
eyes softened. One after another, seven times running,
the shots rang out like cannon fire.

Learoyd had no more bullets in the barrel of his
Colt and was obliged to change magazines.

The eighth body lay absolutely still, but its eyes were shrieking, yelling. He had no wish to die, he had no wish to die yet.

Life! Life! Life! Life! Life!

His lips moved, I thought I heard what sounded like an animal trying to talk. He was looking at me with an expression of unutterable terror. I read in his eyes such a longing for flight, such panic, that I leaned forward to stop Learoyd:

"No!"

The warm brains spattered in my face and I was deafened for several seconds. I saw, though I could not hear, Learoyd fire his pistol at the sky, then fling it away in fury. The Jap's eyes remained wide open; they were still full of horror, but life, more horrifying still, had fled. His face was now one of all those death masks which look the same.

That evening we took a prisoner: a poor devil ravaged by dysentery. It was on that day, too, that I discovered my carnivorous orchid while helping Learoyd look for the Colt he had thrown away. In fact it was a *Nepenthes distillatoria,* which does not belong to the orchid family at all. It was a variety as yet unknown. Back in England, I gave it a name and read a paper on it to the Royal Botanical Society.

Thus began the Battle of the Great Mountain of the Dead—the Battle of Golgotha, as the Australian pilots called it. I was to take part in it for only seven days, because on August 13 I was wounded.

[209]

"Nothing that's happening in this horrible forest has any importance," Dr. Cheng (or Chang) had declared. On August 6, 1945, at 0815 hours (local time), the first atomic bomb exploded over Hiroshima. Sixteen hours later the Americans announced the news to the world, but in our horrible forest we did not hear about it till the 8th.

Neither Learoyd nor I realized the far-reaching consequences of this event. Learoyd hadn't the faintest idea of what an atomic bomb might be, and I gave him a few vague explanations ($E = mc^2$. The cell, composed of atoms, is born, wears out, and dies to be reborn. The atom itself is immortal. If it could be split, however, this eternity would be transformed into considerable energy). The whole thing took no more than an hour's conversation, then our horrible forest closed in on us again.

Terror, despair, madness, crime are all, like man himself, ephemeral; they pass away and disappear. Nothing remains of them unless they have been graven in stone. The Japanese column slowly dissolved; it was

[210]

transformed bit by bit into a fetid stench, into ants, leeches, humus, into blades of grass under the stars, into flies. Of all this there now remains no trace except for a few bullet scratches on the bark of trees.

The Japanese column foundered like a ship broken up in a storm, but the crew remained at the pumps right to the end, and all the time they knew they were going to die. The water kept rising, but they went on pumping. They were still pumping even after they were submerged and it was finished. The Japanese column sank as deep into horror as human nature will allow.

One thing you must know: it's not thirsting after evil, but hungering after bread or rice that makes men damned.

We took further prisoners, wretched, pitiful creatures. One of them spoke English. He enlightened us on the massacre at Tamong Miri. Hunger! The Japanese army was dying of hunger. The legs sliced off, the child's body hacked to pieces did have the significance we had all suspected: hunger.

Learoyd was interrogating. Slowly, in a dull, monotonous voice. He was implacable, unapproachable, so tense he was almost withdrawn. He wanted to know, he wanted full details.

"The rear guard did it all. While searching, they discovered a sack of rice and some ayak, they went berserk." The Jap was rambling on. I wondered whether Learoyd was going to kill him, but I could not tell from his expression. In the end the Jap fell silent, and when Learoyd still pressed him, he said in a strange toneless voice:

[211]

"I've survived, but don't you see that that's why I'm dead already?"

And he did not say another word.

He set off with the other prisoners on the long trip to Cheng's (or Chang's) hospital. There, he was cared for and decently fed. When he began to feel better, he killed himself.

On August 13 I was wounded.

It happened ordinarily enough, and as usual in the jungle, I hardly saw a thing. That evening four or five of us were making our way along a little track running through a ravine, when the forest suddenly crackled viciously. Bits of branches and a shower of bark and stones flew all around me, and I found myself lying dazed in the middle of the track as though I had just been tripped. There was no one in sight, but the bullets were ripping through the grass and sending up earth as they thudded into the ground; some of them ricocheted and whined past me.

I could not feel a thing, but I had an intimation that I had been wounded, and just as this notion sank in, a prodigious instinctive force pushed me to my feet, against all reason or prudence. I just had time to glimpse on my right a Japanese aiming at me. I passed very close to him, certainly within three yards. For a split second I saw his eyes watching me. I rushed on headlong. I heard nothing. I felt nothing. I was in full flight. I staggered. Abruptly I was transfixed by a stab of such violent pain that I barely managed to take two or three more tottering steps and crawl into dense thorny bushes.

The firing started again. A grenade exploded. There was a scream of agony cut short by a second grenade, then silence fell once more. I heard Japanese voices hailing one another close by. I dared not move; I tried to muffle the beating of my heart. My mouth felt as dry and sour as though I had eaten ashes.

It was the dark that saved me, the dark and the weakness of the Japanese. They looked for me for a long time, then I heard them utter some animal cries to form up again, and they disappeared down the track.

I remember the cold, and the rain that fell that night. I remember the rustling, the forest's creaks and groans. I remember the pulsing of my blood, the pain that gnawed at my side. I don't know how long I lay there, unable to move an inch. I had to make a considerable effort to finger my wounds and stop the bleeding; then I dragged myself out of my thorn bushes.

My first night alone in the jungle! I was wounded; all around me I was aware of wild beasts thirsting for warm blood. I fell asleep, or else I fainted. I woke shivering in the rain. I could not move a muscle, I was paralyzed. I, too, was going to be eaten alive. No one would ever find me. No one would put a bullet through my head so that this foul world of ants, of insects with pincers, sightless leeches, might mercifully disappear.

In the morning I dragged myself as far as the trail and struggled along it for two or three miles before running into the patrol which Learoyd had hastily dispatched to look for me. I was empty, devoid of thought, dulled, stupid. I was placed on a stretcher. I was running a high fever. None of this mattered to me. I fell asleep, conscious of a tremendous sensation of swaying and dizziness . . .

I am drifting, sinking, half awakened. Someone gives me something to drink. It's as though I am floating. I feel myself growing heavy. I think I am going to die. Someone gives me an injection.

Days pass. Nights also. Rain. Sun. I am drowning, getting out of my depth. The cold . . .

When I opened my eyes I was in Cheng's (or Chang's) hospital. Japan had surrendered. The war was over.

I spent five days in the hospital, during which the worthy Dr. Cheng (or Chang) deliberated whether he should cut off my leg. (Antibiotics saved it, thank heaven.) The tumult of action, fatigue, rain, cold, sun, hunger, the repellent promiscuity of life among the Muruts, had left me hardly any time to think. For several months I had been nothing but a young dog, barking and running, running and barking, who sometimes at night raised his muzzle to the stars and howled the strange hymn of life. Alone on my bunk, when the pain kept me awake till dawn, I took this opportunity to take stock of my existence.

I was thirty years old. The war was over. I was alive. I asked myself whether I had remained faithful to the image of myself, to that incorruptible young man whom each of us keeps buried in the depths of his conscience and who resembles us like a brother.

Who am I? I asked myself.

I had the feeling that I had not controlled my life, I had submitted to it. Life had seized me and carried me wherever it saw fit.

[215]

As a child I wanted to be a sailor, and I had become a botanist. The great wind of war had brought me back to Borneo. "The wind bloweth where it listeth, and thou hearest the sound thereof, but canst not tell whence it cometh, and whither it goeth." With all the enthusiasm, the splendid hopes of youth, I had embarked on adventure. I had put on all my canvas, the top-gallant and the main-royal, the studding-sails, the ringsails. I had laughed when the masts strained and the shrouds quivered; I had laughed when heavy seas broke over the bridge; I had laughed when the tattered sails were blown away in shreds, like dreams. In those days I felt that I might endure forever or die at once and that this was only fair. The judgment of God. Double or nothing. I might just as well have drained the cup of hemlock to see whether I was innocent and what my fate would be.

I had set out in quest of myself and had lost all my certainties. I was restless, uneasy, my thoughts pell-mell like disordered pieces of a puzzle: one minute I wanted to get up and flee, the next I would have liked to live my life over again and say: I have done this but not that, and this again I never meant to do. I was confused. I was no longer certain. The war was over, I was alive, and that was all.

I don't remember those five days very clearly. I was in great pain and the morphine dulled my senses. Learoyd had come with me; he had to regain his grip on his kingdom, which he had relinquished somewhat since the massacre at Tamong Miri. He was not fond of Cheng and gave the hospital a wide berth in spite of the presence of the two little Japanese nursing sisters. They had both put on weight, they were even lovelier and more alluring.

The taller, the one whom I called mine, performed her duties without seeking to see me or avoid me. Her imperturbable demeanor annoyed me. I pulled her down on top of me one day, while she was changing my dressings, and was quite surprised to find that she responded to my kiss. Her husband, the one who played the *shakuhachi*, had also managed to get posted to the hospital and prowled around us, morose and suspicious. This amused me momentarily; then I relapsed into my gloomy meditations.

Every morning the stony-faced old missionary would come and see me.

"You look tired," he said to me on one of his visits.

I had just spent a sleepless night and was particularly irritable.

"No," I replied, "I feel old. Let me tell you something. I've had all a man can have: youth, power, excitement, and good luck. I've done nothing with them. I've taken and cast aside. I've wasted everything. I feel old."

The old missionary looked at me tranquilly: "You'll get over it. But it's true, you do look tired."

My sleepless night had left me exhausted and elated, as though I had been struggling with the demon. The long wait for dawn had been painful. I was running a temperature, and now I needed to talk.

"You don't understand. I'm old, I haven't lived, I've merely taken advantage of life. Life is like war, it devastates everything. Living means fighting. Look at a tree towering up into the sky; according to the law of gravity it ought to creep over the rocks like lichen, but it towers up, 180 feet tall. Then think of a whole forest!"

I stopped talking. My leg and hip were aching, but above all I felt I was not succeeding in expressing the emotion that gripped me. The old man who expected nothing from death "except the mercy of God" smiled faintly. "Yes, God's creation is marvelous."

"No, that's nothing to do with it. Let me tell you something—we're all going to die, not sleep and dream. No, everything will be finished, there'll be nothing afterward. If we haven't fought in life, then there's nothing unfair about our death, any more than it's unfair for the fatted calf to be led to the slaughterhouse. What is the point of courage? What is the point of bravery in the face of death if one has shown cowardice in the face of life? Our death has to be an injustice!"

I don't know if these were the actual words I used. I was vehement and no doubt incoherent, I was shaking with fever, but I remember this conversation clearly; in fact it is the only clear recollection I have of those five hazy days. The old man with the worn stony mask looked at me with a benevolence I found unbearable.

"At first men are dazzled by life," he said, "then bit by bit they feel doubt creeping in. Man is simpler and more naïve than one thinks, you know. Man is born, suffers and dies, but what about his soul? His soul is a mystery, the soul is immense, it's on the scale of . . . the world, the universe. It's the battlefield between Satan and God. God is never wholly given except to children."

[218]

The pious old fool hasn't understood a thing, I thought, and his alleged knowledge of life is just hot air.

"Each time a creature is born," I declared peremptorily, "a whole world, with its sun, stars, and grass blades, comes into being and gradually takes on its particular coloring, its individual light and shade. Each time a creature dies, his whole world, with its sun, stars, and grass blades, disappears forever. The disappearance of these worlds is scandalous, but the more rich and colorful the world the greater the scandal. So let's create a mighty scandal, and may God be ashamed."

The death of the eighth Japanese lying paralyzed on the trail on Golgotha already seemed to me an injustice and a crying scandal because his world was rich; he wanted to live out his agony for a few hours yet, for all that he was helpless and being eaten alive. The colors of Learoyd's world—Learoyd who had won a kingdom and driven out God—were brighter than mine, his sun more ardent. He had roused an ancient people from their lethargy and proclaimed the return of the days of high adventure. He was the salt in the rice, as Gwai had said.

I announced my decision to the startled old missionary: "I'm not going back. I'm going to stay with Learoyd."

"You're feverish, you must calm down," he muttered.

Feverish! It was my imagination that was feverish, my imagination that needed calming down. In fact I was not completely mad, but I was very ill.

On the fourth day Anderson came down from the

radio station to tell me that Fergusson was coming to fetch me in the morning.

"He also wants to see Learoyd. He insisted. He said, 'That's an order.' "

During the night, Learoyd arrived, followed by his shadow, Gwai the Silent, who was carrying a torch. It was a lovely cool night with a gentle breeze blowing off the torrent; my temperature had fallen slightly and I was dozing. In the blaze of the red flame crackling with sparks and the coils of black smoke, their sudden appearance had something supernatural about it. I didn't recognize them for a moment.

"This is the parting of the ways. I've come to say goodbye," Learoyd said calmly.

I was still doped with morphine and my mind was working slowly.

"But I'm not leaving. Besides, Fergusson wants to see you tomorrow," I replied.

"Tomorrow I won't be here."

"But what about Fergusson?"

"I don't want to see him."

A puff of wind made the flame leap up and the smoke swirl in a shower of sparks. Gwai's bronze skin glistened as though it were wet. I sat up on my bunk.

"Learoyd, I'm not leaving. I've decided to stay with you. You'll need me, it's going to be tough."

Learoyd looked at me. I could see nothing but a pair of unwavering gray eyes in the flickering light. He was silent for a long time; then he said slowly, "You know damn well you're going to leave."

I felt as though I'd had the wind knocked out of me.

[220]

"Goodbye," he added. "I like you. Whatever you may do, you're my friend."

He shook hands and marched out at once. This was night indeed.

Fergusson's plane landed next day, as soon as the morning mist had lifted.

The matter was summarily dealt with. Fergusson was furious because Learoyd, "that mad Irishman of yours," was not there. He managed to keep himself in check when I told him I wanted to stay on, merely putting a hand on my forehead to check my temperature, but he literally exploded when Anderson announced timidly that he had no intention of leaving either. It was a rage to end all rages, and he swore shamelessly. Truu Big-Belly-Button and his wife, the six-fingered idiot, who happened to be with Anderson, shot off like startled hares. Cheng (or Chang), his broad Chinese face beaming, tactfully withdrew. The dogs began to bark.

Fergusson suddenly calmed down and assumed that icy tone that used to impress even the toughest bastards at Great Barrier Reef.

"In the first place, who the hell are you?"

"I'm Ander . . . er . . . Signal Sergeant Anderson, sir," Anderson stammered, putting matters right.

"Right. You'll be hearing more about this. Meanwhile I give you ten minutes. I want you to report here with your kit. You're coming with us."

The airplane took off toward eleven o'clock. The hot air shimmered in the sun. The forest looked impassive. Great menacing cumulus clouds were piling up in the south, beyond the heights. Fergusson was muttering to

[221]

himself. Anderson had his nose glued to the plexiglass of the cabin. Lying on my stretcher, I caught a glimpse of the valley as the plane banked steeply to gain height before setting course for Labuan. I realized then how sad I was.

At Labuan there was cool beer and a gentle sea breeze. I was struck by the robust vitality of everyone I saw. I was given a pair of pajamas that had a freshly laundered smell and was promptly transferred to Morotai to be operated on.

The war was over. Armstrong and the Australians of the
9th Division had received the surrender of the Japanese
entrenched on the plantation, but there was still some
fighting in the east; for another month or more the
phantom column and a few other dying remnants of the
Japanese Army, red with blood and black with despair,
would eat human flesh in order to keep alive and continue the fight.

The Air Force carried out a few more sorties for our
benefit; then all military activity ceased. Australian
GHQ refused to risk any more lives. One after another
my instructors were recalled. By mid-September the only
ones left were Armstrong, two radio operators, and
Conklin, deep in the jungle, who was turning a deaf
ear.

The Japanese still refused to surrender; some DC3s
dropped leaflets to them with the text of the Emperor's
speech; some Muruts were sent to them with messages,
but they were killed (and perhaps eaten); an officer
prisoner was even dispatched in an attempt to convince

them: all to no avail. Slowly, day by day, they worked their way farther west, and the valleys at the end of the world still echoed with tragic bugle calls and the sound of rifle fire.

Fergusson was assailed on all sides. The Dutch were demanding the immediate evacuation of Sergeant Learoyd from their colony. The Australians were withdrawing their troops. The British Administration was insisting on all weapons being handed in and all irregular formations being disbanded. The war was over, everything was to revert to normal.

We were gradually losing control of the Murut territory. Learoyd had disappeared; he maintained only occasional cautious contact with Armstrong. Senghir was full of good will, but he was far from enjoying unanimous support among the tribes of the west; his authority was even questioned in his own village, where the young warriors of the militia remained fervent partisans of the kingdom. As soon as the Japanese on the Sapong Estate had capitulated, the refugees poured back to the coast.

The Muruts joined forces among themselves, and it soon became clear that they now existed as a nation and were not willing to accept their prewar situation. The reports from Armstrong, who was grappling on the spot with countless difficulties, left this in no doubt: there would be no further division between the British in the west and the Dutch in the east; the Muruts would defend their unity and independence by force of arms. I don't know what political agreements there were at top level between the Australians, the British, and the

Dutch under the shadow of MacArthur, but this news acted like a bomb. There was a general outcry.

In mid-September, on his way back from a stormy meeting with the Dutch at Brisbane, Fergusson stopped off at Morotai to see me. I was still in the hospital, but I had calmed down a little. The darkness of the forest, so merciless to human weakness, the red Sembakung, the gloomy, hopeless sky, the savage hordes of Comanches, the beating of the war gongs, the buzzing of the flies around hanged men, the sound and fury of the sunken valleys, had been blotted out. The peaceful, rather colorless course of life had reclaimed me: cool beer, sea bathing, English nurses.

I no longer sneered insolently at respectable people; I drank in moderation; I was slothful. Lolling in pajamas in a planter's chair, I dreamed of buying a Malayan prahu and sailing back alone to England. I worked out how many pounds of rice and dried fish I would need to take with me. I selected my ports of call: the Macassar Strait, the Sunda Strait, Ceylon, the Maldives; I was hesitating between the route of the tea clippers, of the *Cutty Sark*—the Cape and the South Atlantic—or Aden and the Red Sea.

"It's a hell of a mess. We can't allow that lunatic to stick his neck out any longer," Fergusson concluded, after describing the situation to me.

There was long silence. Fergusson, with his tired gaze, sat facing me; behind him, beyond the white line of surf, the sun shimmered on a dazzling blue sea.

"He's not entirely to blame," I said at last. "After all, the Muruts . . ."

[225]

"I know," the old colonel broke in. "I know, I know. No, I don't know. I don't know anything. I'm a soldier. You don't know anything either. To hell with imagination, it leads us into temptation. It whispers in our ears and gives us ideas that would lead us straight to perdition if we didn't watch out. We're soldiers, we've chosen to believe in simple things. We'll do what's asked of us, and knowing the vanity of human undertakings and how the best laid schemes can gang agley, may God preserve us."

Since I made no reply, he went on: "There's no salvation if one doesn't toe the line, believe me."

His tanned face was impassive, as though carved in seasoned oak. His deep voice sounded firm and resolute, as though expressing certainties, yet I sensed in it the quiver of an uneasy doubt.

"Learoyd won't toe the line," I said, shaking my head.

"He will, poor devil, one way or the other he will. No one ever moves very far out of line, you know. When you're young you sometimes think you're blazing a trail—you don't notice it's a beaten track. You want to be different, to be . . . better or worse, more . . . well, different, eh? Unique! So you forge straight ahead, possessed by the demon in your soul. Often it's a woman who brings you back in line. Or else it's life. Two or three blows from life. Ha! Ha! Ha!"

A corner of the veil had lifted for a moment, revealing an unexpected Colonel Fergusson, but I was not sure of what I thought I had glimpsed. He turned toward the sea. The languid breeze was laden with scents of salt and iodine. Distantly there came the happy laughter of a nurse on the beach, punctuated by the deeper voice of a man. Life seemed sweet, calm, and voluptuous.

"In a month's time the northeasterly monsoon will be back," Fergusson said suddenly, out of the blue. "Listen, you know him best—what can we do?"

"For him, nothing."

"You mean there's really nothing we can do? Poor devil!" Fergusson repeated.

"Well . . ."

I knew Fergusson was right, that everyone was right, that one must be reasonable, that "life is not all beer and skittles," as my father's old housekeeper used to say. I hesitated all the same. I would rather have found myself in the middle of the Indian Ocean in bad weather aboard my prahu, with my rice and my dried fish, than do what I was going to do.

"Well, there's the salt. Without salt the revolt will fizzle out in three months. He told me so himself."

At the end of the month, still convalescent, I went back to Labuan. The situation had deteriorated considerably. On September 28 our last radio station sent a laconic message: "We're pulling out." On October 12 Armstrong and his two operators turned up at Tomani. Armstrong had a message from Learoyd: "Leave us alone and we'll leave you alone."

All the tracks leading into the interior were already

blocked with arrows and thorn bushes. One of our routine patrols, guided by some Red Dogs, was brought to a halt on the Upper Tungkalis.

"Two or three bullets whistled twenty feet over our heads," the NCO in charge reported. "You couldn't see a thing, but our savages were yelling like men possessed. They were arguing with the ones on the other side. The interpreter told me it was impossible to advance further. He kept repeating, 'They not bad men, we no advance.' But he seemed to be in a blue funk. Since my orders were to avoid clashes with the civilians and my radio was out of action, I decided to return."

There were further incidents of this sort.

On the 15th a convoy of a hundred or so Japanese prisoners—living skeletons—arrived at Tomani. The Comanche escort tried to exchange some gold dust for salt—unsuccessfully, for Fergusson had issued his orders. The Comanches were disarmed and allowed to return to their homes.

On the 17th Conklin, emaciated but in high spirits and festooned with Japanese swords, emerged from the jungle on the banks of the River Padas. He knew nothing about our difficulties. On the 5th he had still been fighting against the phantom column. Learoyd had come to fetch him; they had had "one hell of a binge, with girls, ayak—the lot." Then three of his "desert rats" had accompanied him to the river, feasting in every longhouse they encountered along the track. His liver was in such poor shape that he had to spend a fortnight in the hospital.

On the east coast the Dutch, who were gradually

taking over from the Australians of Tarakan, were not able to advance far enough up the Sembakung delta to penetrate the Plain of Elephants.

Learoyd's Murut kingdom was now completely cut off from the rest of the world.

The first northeasterly breezes reached Labuan, wafting huge jagged clouds the color of lead over a sea that had turned green. Day by day the dark red sunsets looked more and more like the death agony of a lifeless planet. The nights became humid and sultry. I suggested to Fergusson that I should have a final meeting with Learoyd and try . . .

"Try what?" he growled grumpily.

"I don't know, convince him that he can't . . ."

"He's a stubborn mule. He won't listen."

The scheme was adopted, however, and a DC3 was put at the disposal of Special Forces.

"All right, go ahead. At least we'll know what's happening back there," Fergusson concluded. He had no illusions.

On October 21 I took off from the airfield of Victoria Harbor. For the third time I was going to jump into the heart of Borneo.

The forest . . . forest . . . forest . . . There were men in the darkness, beneath that vault so tranquil, motionless, impenetrable, huge, and beautiful; perhaps the last Japanese in the process of dying, all alone. The red Sembakung, dazzling as a mirror reflecting the sun, the valley to the east under a transparent mist, our landing

[229]

strip, invaded by the undergrowth, the rice fields . . .

Learoyd was not there. I spent two very pleasant days with Gwai in the longhouse, being made much of by all my friends, Truu Big-Belly-Button and Anderson's gang of "Dynamo-Comanches." It was almost like the good old days, before the landing at Tarakan.

There were some Japanese living in my former command post, halfway to the dismantled radio station. They worked in the rice fields and on the irrigation canals. In the evening they played a little music and came to drink ayak under the veranda.

I went for walks in the Forest of the Spirits. I bathed in the torrent. Yoo was no longer there, nor the little prince with the gray eyes, but in the golden glory of the morning there were still lovely young girls of bronze, slim and naked, their heads held high, polishing the skin of their thighs with pebbles.

Once again I saw Learoyd the Magnificent, lean and tall, with his tattoo mark and his hair red as revolt. He was tougher, less talkative, more enigmatic; even his eyes seemed grayer than before the massacre at Tamong Miri, but he looked happy once more. He was living with the little Japanese nurse, who had refused to leave when Cheng's hospital was withdrawn at the end of August. As soon as I saw him again I realized the uselessness of my mission.

On my way back to Tomani, I called in on Senghir, whom I found motionless, watchful, patient as a coiled cobra in the ruins of his old house. The northeasterly monsoon had passed over the Crocker Range, crossed the River Padas, and reached the Sembakung. The first clouds, huge, black, and heavy, their bellies tinged with sulphur, were blotting out the sun. A menacing darkness hovered over the stifling valley.

"A dark sky does not clear without a storm. We can do nothing: he is a man who thinks he's God."

PART THREE

The
Return
of the
Northeasterly
Monsoon

"I know thy works, that thou hast a
name, that thou livest, and art dead."

APOCALYPSE *III:1*

I had left Learoyd a king. Three months later, in a little military outpost east of Tomani, I saw him a prisoner, bleeding and mute. "He was already dead," the Japanese colonel would have said.

I shall never forget his eyes that day. They gazed at me, they had no expression, and this was perhaps more frightening than the emptiness I had seen in them on that rainy morning of the massacre at Tamong Miri.

He was locked up in a cell, a sort of blockhouse made of damp logs. The sergeant had shouted, "Stand up!" He had risen slowly to his feet. His face was swollen, his long red hair matted with fresh blood and blackened clots. He did not say a word. He did not reply to our questions. I was never again to hear the sound of his voice.

There he stood, upright, motionless. He gazed at me. Was he judging me, perhaps? I don't know. He gazed at me, his eyes a blank. Nothingness, gray, cold, vacant.

"Who knocked him about like that?" Fergusson asked at last.

"Well, sir, it's the—it was the men, sir," the sergeant stammered sheepishly.

Fergusson's icy silence disconcerted him still further.

"I wasn't there, sir. I was at Tomani when the savages brought him in, him and the Jap. He refused to speak, sir, like now. The men gave him a bit of a pasting. After all, he's a deserter."

Fergusson's anger cracked like a whiplash. I suddenly recognized the boss of the good old days at Great Barrier Reef.

"You had no right. You're a disgrace to the army. You deserve to be stripped."

The wretched sergeant was petrified. Learoyd had not moved, his gaze had switched for a moment to Fergusson, then returned to rest on me, insistent, calm, devoid of thought and devoid of hope. I had the impression of a message not getting through: was he inwardly despising the sentimentality which made me deplore the cruelty of his fate?

"Oh, God!" Fergusson muttered when we were outside again in the muddy compound.

"We must forgive him. We all need to be forgiven," he went on, without my knowing whether he was referring to the sergeant or to Learoyd.

The day was fading, broad bands of red streaking the sky in the west. The moisture-laden wind teased out long, fierce, black clouds. The wild dog, the only surviving dog in this silent valley, started howling. He must have been prowling around the post, because we heard him again during the night.

We had waited three months, Fergusson and I, bowing before the storm. There was nothing else we could do. My blockade was effective, not a grain of salt got through to the Murut kingdom. The Red Dogs had been bought, and Learoyd did not have enough gold dust to suborn them. His men, denounced by the populace at Tomani and in the north, were arrested while trying to organize a smuggling operation.

We had waited three months. I remember the feverish days and the sultry nights, the enervating heat and the everlasting rain of the northeasterly monsoon. Fergusson remained unperturbed. Every evening he went for a swim. He swam straight toward the open sea and did not return until nightfall.

"We must wait," he kept saying. "A chicken can still run about for some time after its head has been cut off."

Borneo was settling down to peace. The last groups of Japanese, starving and terrified, surrendered. The Australians repatriated their troops. The Civil Administration gradually took over. Everything was in short supply, everything was in ruins in this most distant, forgotten, and war-ravaged part of the British Commonwealth. Everything had to be restarted from scratch.

We got down to work with a will. We had faith in the necessity and justice of our task, but beyond the River Padas, behind the blue hills, in the darkness of the jungle, the Kingdom of the Three Forests, Learoyd's impregnable citadel, still evaded our laws.

"We must wait," said Fergusson.

The affair assumed ridiculous proportions. Some wanted to drop paratroops to seize "the mad Irishman," dead or alive. Others suggested legally appointing him headman of a Murut district. Still others thought of

[237]

putting a price on his head. There were some unfortunate incidents on the new frontier, an exchange of shots, the disappearance of a lieutenant who was handed back to us disarmed a few days later. (He had gone off to hunt wild boar and had ventured too far.)

The most hair-raising stories got about: Learoyd was a member of the Communist Party; he had discovered a gold mine, or a ruby mine; he had rallied the last Japanese stragglers to form a private army of his own. In London the Labour Government, which had been in power since July 25, preoccupied by the difficult situation in Java and French Indochina, was getting worried. We were honored with a visit from two Members of Parliament on a fact-finding mission.

"We must wait," Fergusson told them.

The Dutch never stopped complaining and pestering us with claims. They held us responsible for the situation. One of their administrators and a small troop of soldiers had been fired upon while moving up the Sembakung. There had been some killed and wounded. In reprisal they had bombed a village with Dakotas and a Catalina seaplane. I knew the village they bombed; it had already been burned by the Japanese in 1943. Its militia had tracked down the famous phantom column south of the Plain of Elephants and had fought valiantly at the Battle of Leopard Pass. Learoyd had a charming girl friend there, "fashioned by the spirits," who used to laugh all night when he was with her, preventing me from sleeping.

I was furious; these reprisals were both stupid and unjust. Fergusson protested violently, and our relations with the Dutch deteriorated still further. It was worse when they arrested some Muruts who were buying salt in a fishing village east of Tarakan with gold sovereigns. Gold sovereigns! The treachery of British Special Forces was confirmed! The sovereigns were obviously those I had so liberally distributed to the handsome lads of the kingdom and which Learoyd must have recovered, but the Dutch administration preferred to believe we were financing a rebellion.

Wait, wait, wait, we must wait.

"I don't see what else we can do. We're not going to start a war in the jungle. And the Dutch have their hands full already with Java and Sumatra."

Fergusson remained unperturbed. He was a rampart, a bastion that withstood every assault. Yet behind this mask of certainty, a doubt was slowly pursuing its blind course until that day in October 1946 when, just as the solution to a difficult problem appears suddenly obvious and crystal clear, Fergusson threw himself overboard.

I could have perceived certain signs of this undermining activity in the silence of his soul if I had been more on the alert. He had become less talkative, and every day he read the Bible. In the evenings he swam longer and longer, going farther and farther out, no matter what the weather. I never went with him, I couldn't have, but sometimes I used to wait for him anxiously on the beach.

"You're not afraid of being unable to get back to shore?" I asked him one night when light seemed to have vanished utterly from the world.

His voice was partly drowned by the sound of the

[239]

invisible surf. "Swim far out . . . the more death horrifies me . . . Extremely stimulating . . ."

A little later, back in the bungalow, he said, "What if this kingdom were to last, eh?"

"Well, we . . ." I faltered.

"Well, there'd be one kingdom more under the sun. That's all!"

At the beginning of December our patience was at last rewarded: three longhouses west of the Tungkalis came over to our side. It was not much of a victory; these three villages, traditionally sympathetic to the Red Dogs, had never really been an integral part of the kingdom; but this was the first tangible evidence of the efficacy of our blockade. Since we were unable to control the distribution of salt so deep in the interior, the three villages were resettled on the banks of the Padas, between Tomani and the Sapong Estate, under the protection of the army. There was no incident: the women, children, and old men arrived safely. The young warriors had preferred to join Learoyd's militias.

During the second fortnight of December a runner from Senghir arrived at Tomani and asked to see us. The news he brought was almost unbelievable: Learoyd was preparing a raid down to the coast, in Dutch territory, through the Plain of Elephants. His shock troops, who were to clear the way for the salt gatherers, would be Japanese volunteers under the command of a great chieftain "whose sword struck before men saw the flash of it." We passed on all this information to the Dutch at Tarakan.

[240]

The Army took the necessary steps. The Navy patrolled the east coast and the delta of the Sembakung. The last RAAF Beaufighters were ordered to stand by.

During the night of Christmas Eve a great battle took place east of Tarakan, on the outskirts of a fishing village. For a moment it looked as though fortune, which hangs by a thread, was going to favor Learoyd's enterprise. Though they had been reported two days earlier by some Chinese lumbermen, his shock troops crossed the mangrove swamp without being spotted and emerged on the coast. It was a fisherman who gave the alarm. The beach was promptly pounded foot by foot by naval artillery and by the Air Force. Everything that could fly took off with a load of bombs, came back and touched down to reload, then flew out again in an unending cycle. The first village blazed like a torch.

On Christmas morning Learoyd's forces, decimated and defeated, withdrew into the forest. The Dutch patrols sent in after them ran into booby traps as diabolical as any Conklin could have devised. They suffered some losses and soon abandoned the pursuit. The rising sun revealed forty or so charred bodies on the beach and in the mangrove swamp. Twenty Japanese soldiers and two Comanches from Tamong Miri who had acted as guides were taken prisoner. Their interrogation at last shed some light on what was happening in the kingdom, and we were dumbfounded by what we heard.

On October 10 or 11 Learoyd had won over the colonel commanding the last survivors of the phantom column. The colonel told his men that they were going to stay peacefully in this country for a certain length of

[241]

time to avoid being taken prisoner by the Australians. The nightmare was over! The Japanese soldiers, at death's door and almost crazed with despair and misery, were fed and tended by the Murut warriors. After the months of horror, darkness, and bloodshed, it seems that Japanese and Muruts felt the need to love one another, to warm themselves side by side in the sun. It seems that a surge of compassion and generosity illumined the forest darkness. It seems that the lion and the lamb lay down together.

A great feast was held on the cold ashes of Tamong Miri to celebrate the return of the good spirits of the northeasterly wind, the moist wind of life. The Japanese soldiers worked in the paddy fields, improved the irrigation system, organized the pig breeding, widened some of the tracks, and even built a suspension bridge over the Sembakung! They felt free and useful.

Then the salt began to fail. There were complaints and quarrels. The rice was insipid, the meat had a sweetish taste. The youngest children fell ill and some of them died. There were tears and lamentations. Learoyd then decided to march to the coast, and the night of Christmas Eve was the result. This—*this*—is what the twenty Japanese and the guides from Tamong Miri told us.

In reprisal the Dutch, despite our protests, burned down a longhouse with their DC3s, but they no longer ventured into the Plain of Elephants. Learoyd's raid had cost them a dozen dead, including three white officers. In spite of the victory they were in a very ugly mood.

[242]

Once again we had to wait. Fergusson remained apparently unperturbed.

"Now it's the beginning of the end. We've won," he said bitterly, after reading the report from Tarakan.

He dispatched back into the interior a few of the Comanches arrested at Tomani, telling them that we would lift the salt blockade as soon as Learoyd and the Japanese colonel had been handed over to us.

We waited.

And throughout the time of waiting the forest was perfectly calm and silent. Impassive and impenetrable, with infinite patience, it had closed in on the drama being enacted in the distant valleys. I often had a touch of fever at this time, which left me restless, tense, and irritable, and exasperated Fergusson.

"Stop fidgeting about like that. So much energy is disgusting."

It was not until February 3 that it was finished. A radioman roused me with a message from Tomani: "The crown and sabre were handed over to us last night."

I rushed across to Fergusson: "It's all over. We've got them."

The sole survivor of the massacre of the dogs was howling in the twilight. After leaving Learoyd, we crossed the muddy compound to the opposite block-house in which the Japanese colonel was imprisoned. He was a skinny little man of about fifty, with close-cropped hair and a brisk manner. He rattled off his name, rank,

[243]

and regimental number. His excellent English had a faintly throaty accent.

The sergeant in command of the post hauled a frightened corporal before us.

"He was the one in charge, sir. I was at Tomani."

"I know. You said so before," Fergusson growled. Then, turning to the corporal, he asked, "How did it happen?"

"Well, sir, it's like this. The savages turned up at sundown. It was raining. They dumped them just outside the door, like a couple of parcels, and waited without saying a word. I went out to see what they wanted. Their chief, at least I think it was their chief, said he'd had a bellyful. Well, he said he'd had enough, that it was all the fault of these two here, and that they wanted some salt. I checked to see if these were the men we were after, and I gave them a couple of hundred-pound sacks, as agreed."

The Japanese colonel, whom we had temporarily forgotten, interrupted the corporal: "No, it wasn't quite like that."

Fergusson swung around. I thought he was going to give the prisoner a good dressing down, but he merely looked at him for a moment, then asked calmly: "How did it happen?"

"Gwai, Ballang Gwai, handed us over. We were both strung up to a bamboo pole. When this . . . when the corporal arrived, Ballang Gwai made a little speech in English."

"What did he say?"

"He said—I remember his very words. It was a fine

[244]

speech, very sad—he said, 'We are an old people, we are worn out, we want peace and salt.' Then he added, 'This man here is my brother, the king, and the other one is our sword. Our king is the red flame which has set the whole forest on fire.' And he repeated once more, 'We are an old people, we are worn out, we want peace and salt.' I don't know how he had learned his speech, but he knew it by heart and recited it like a schoolboy."

"Thank you."

Fergusson turned back to the corporal. "And are you responsible for Learoyd's being in that state?"

Fergusson's voice sounded terrifying to me, and evidently to the corporal as well, for he at once defended himself: "Sir, the men were provoked, sir. They were firing over our heads, we even had one man wounded, so . . ."

"One man wounded?" Fergusson interjected. "Who? I know nothing about this. When? Who was the man?"

"What I mean, sir, Maxi, Maxi Laurens, sir, in November, he fell down on the Tomani track. But even so they did fire over our heads, sir, twice."

The corporal was losing the thread of his feeble explanations. Fergusson shrugged his shoulders.

The Japanese colonel went on quietly, "They untied us after Gwai went off with his salt. They didn't lay a finger on me, but him . . . first of all they mocked him. He couldn't stand upright. His joints were stiff. He refused to speak, so they started beating him and calling him the King of—the King of Cunts, I believe. They put a helmet on his head, jeering: 'Here's your crown.' "

"All right, all right," Fergusson grunted.

[245]

The Japanese colonel's interference had upset him; what had this prisoner to do with it? He regretted having interrogated the corporal in front of him. I fancied I had detected a derisive glint in the colonel's eyes, as though, even as a prisoner, he was satisfied he had scored a point or two. We went out into the compound. The wild dog was no longer howling. Darkness had fallen indeed.

We spent the night in the outpost. The pilot who had managed to land us on the Tomani airstrip despite the driving rain and fog refused to take off in the dark. Fergusson gave orders for Learoyd's wounds to be dressed. The two prisoners were then transferred to more comfortable quarters and a sentry posted outside their door. The rain pattered on the corrugated iron roof.

Fergusson took a solitary turn in the compound, with the same insistence he displayed in swimming every evening to the point of exhaustion. I felt cold and ill, as though I were in for another bout of fever. I drew close to a fire under a shelter. The reddish smoke spiraled up toward the dark sky; every so often a gust of damp wind blew it into my eyes and I wept.

Later on, when we were all asleep, a cry like a call for help rent the silence of the night and the mad dog replied from a distance with a bloodcurdling howl.

It was only Learoyd having nightmares again.

The Japanese colonel was sentenced to be hanged as a war criminal by a military tribunal. Learoyd, called as a witness, refused to speak. From far off, in the box, he looked as vague as a ghost and as still as a stone. This was the last time I saw him. Fergusson had applied for his trial to take place later in England.

On the eve of his execution the colonel expressed a desire to see me. Nothing had been said at his trial about what had happened in the forgotten valleys of the interior during the three months' isolation. Learoyd had not opened his mouth and the colonel himself, charged *inter alia* for his acknowledged participation in the rebellion, had not been exactly enlightening.

I was curious to know what he wanted to tell me and therefore I agreed to his request.

"I sent for you, I'm sorry, I mean I asked if you would be good enough to come and see me, because . . . you know this is my last night, don't you?"

I nodded. He must have sensed my embarrassment at

seeing him stoop to sentimentality, because he went on at once to reassure me.

"Don't worry, I'm not going to bother you with my . . . with that. No! Learoyd told me you were a friend. He hasn't said a thing since 'You too, Gwai.' Those were his last words. That was the last time I heard the sound of his voice. Even when the corporal and the soldier beat him up he didn't say a word, he didn't even protest. He was like a stone. Ever since, he has been unfeeling as a stone.

"I've seen it happen before. It's quite common, you know. At Tarakan, in 1943, I had to have some Chinese bandits shot, some Chinese resistance fighters, I should say. There were fifteen of them. All stones. All but one.

"Have you ever had a man shot? It's an experience, for a soldier. You know, they stand on the edge of the trench of their own accord. They seem full of good will. They look at you, they seem as though they're still alive, but they're already dead. All of them. All but one. He struggled.

"Life, you know, the terrible thirst for life. Yet he was an old man. Learoyd too is already dead. Would you like to hear how it happened?"

I was still wary of the colonel. I did not quite see what he was driving at. There was a strange light in his eyes. I was afraid of being duped.

I replied casually, "What for? Do you want to salve your conscience?"

"You're very young. I too am dead, you see." He spoke in Japanese, then translated: " 'I only wish to rest until the end. I'm thinking of my Emperor . . . and of roses.' Those were the last words of the great Admiral Togo, the victor of Tsushima."

"Why didn't you speak at the trial? It's too late now."

"Too late for what?"

"Too late, I don't know, too late to change anything," I said.

"You don't understand. It doesn't matter. Excuse me." He turned toward the door of his cell and shouted in a loud voice "Guard!"

When the sentry appeared, he rose to his feet and said, "The conversation is at an end. You may . . ."

"No," I said hurriedly. "No. Bring us a pot of coffee and two cups, please."

"But, sir," the sentry began.

"I know," I said, "but tonight is different."

"Yes, sir, very good, sir," the sentry said and marched off.

"Excuse me, Colonel, I'd like you to tell me about it."

The Japanese colonel had watched the sentry's indecision with a serene, mocking smile on his face.

"They're afraid I might commit suicide, hara-kiri, they call it. They're wrong, it's only suicide—hara-kiri is a ceremony. Many . . . war criminals have tried to commit suicide. They are sent to the hospital to make sure they're in a fit state to take their punishment."

"Did you ever feel like committing suicide?"

He hesitated. "No—at least—I'll tell you. Many of my soldiers hanged themselves from despair. I may as well let myself be hanged by the British."

"Justice?"

[249]

"Don't talk to me of justice! I'm defeated and I'm tired, that's all. I'm old. No, it's not a question of age. The old Chinese bandit, you know, struggled like a demon. He wept and reviled the world. He was very old. No, I'm tired, very tired, and then—how can I put it?"

He remained pensive for a moment. "A long time ago, in 1938, in Shanghai, another old Chinaman told me a story, an edifying story. Listen to this!

"Once upon a time there was an emperor—or was it a king? It doesn't matter. The lord and master of a tiny fragment of the surface of the earth. He was old and ill, and he knew that his end was near. He had a son who was very young and very handsome. One night, when he felt particularly weak, the old king summoned to his bedside an old madman who was regarded as a sage throughout the length and breadth of the kingdom and said to him, 'Before I hand over my throne to my son, I want you to teach him wisdom, I want him to know what I do not know, I want him to know the nature and condition of man.'

" 'O my beloved master,' replied the old madman who was regarded as a sage, 'the nature of man is still a secret to me. I don't know it.'

" 'Then teach him the condition of man upon earth.'

" 'O master of my life, that is a fearful discovery which few men dare to face.'

" 'I wish it,' the king insisted. 'Make haste, I give you one moon's time. Do what is needed.'

"That very night the old madman who was regarded as a sage carried off the king's son, had him put in chains

[250]

and flung into a dismal dungeon where a vast number of unfortunates already languished. Every day a deaf-and-dumb executioner, masked and clad in red, would come into the dungeon and seize some of the prisoners, whom he butchered in front of the rest.

"Every day he came back. Sometimes he was blindfolded and chose at random, sometimes he advanced firmly upon his victim, sometimes his gaze wandered a long while and appeared to hesitate, but always the chosen victims were put to death, rapidly, or slowly after a prolonged agony. It even happened that he would spare one whom he had already maimed, only to finish him off the next day.

"Every day fresh prisoners were flung into the dungeon, and every day the executioner levied his tribute. At the end of a moon the old madman who was regarded as a sage came to fetch the king's son. He was just releasing him from his chains when the executioner clad in red entered the dungeon. That day the executioner was blindfolded and chose at random. His inflexible grip fastened on the old madman who was regarded as a sage, and he dragged him to the block despite his howls and entreaties."

"What a horrible story!" I remarked after a moment's silence.

"It's the story of the human condition. I'm settled, I know the executioner has looked me in the eye and that my turn has come. But what about you? Maybe, presently, when he comes to fetch me, he'll choose you as well. Who knows?"

[251]

The colonel peered at me, and once again there was that faint smile, that serene and mischievous gleam in his eyes.

"The venerable Chinese who told me that story used to smoke opium. He too was a madman who was regarded as a sage. When he was deprived of his drug he showed the most appalling cowardice. You see, death is not so terrible. What's terrible is despair. The fate of the king's son . . ."

He winced and leaned solemnly toward me.

"Listen, you're young and I don't know what the world holds in store for you, but beware of the return of the days when men plumb the depths of despair, for no one then can tell what he'll discover in himself: gold-dust or a handful of mud. The sentence will be final and there'll be no appeal."

His voice sank to a strained whisper.

"I have sometimes frightened myself . . . One mustn't sink too deep into the inner darkness, one mustn't plunge into the murky waters of the accursed swamp: monsters are there, underneath, lurking. One mustn't."

He remained for a moment, head bowed toward the ground, then straightened up. The bare electric light bulb hanging from a wire in the middle of the room once more illumined his old soldier's face. He had recovered his serenity.

"One always says too much. Enough of this, it's Learoyd we must talk about. He told me you wanted to rob him of his kingdom at first. I also thought of it. But neither you nor I would have known what to do with it."

I spent the whole night listening to the Japanese

colonel and drinking coffee. He told me how Learoyd had come to find him during the night of October 10, "unarmed, almost as naked as the day he emerged from his mother's womb, and with a tin of corned beef." How "in spite of the darkness of my soul" he had not had him shot. "Perhaps because of his red hair plastered to his head like seaweed? (It was raining, naturally.) Perhaps because he looked more like a dream than a man? Perhaps because he was as emaciated and pitiful as we were? I don't know."

Learoyd had lit a great fire which illuminated the jungle. The first fire in four months. The soldiers scattered in the darkness approached slowly, "still wary, but drawn like moths toward the light." Soon there were a hundred of them, mute and motionless, huddled together for warmth. Then Learoyd spoke of the Kingdom of the Three Forests.

"I believed him, I swear I believed him!" the colonel exclaimed. "Next day we ate some cooked rice, hot, and the flesh of . . . of animals. And then there was the sun. Sun, sky, clouds. And the wind on the heights. And stars the following night."

An extraordinary moment, undoubtedly. I could imagine it.

"I felt like a *ronin*—you know, those Samurais without masters who put their swords at the service of the peasants. At first, of course, I wanted to rob him of his kingdom. Ha! Rob him of what? I ask you! There was nothing—just wind and rain. Nothing to rob him of, you see. And yet it was a fine kingdom . . .

"There was the salt.

[253]

"He held out as long as he could. It was Gwai, his brother, who dealt the death blow, who tied us up.

"You see, his people had abandoned him halfway. Perhaps it's better like this."

At 7:30 in the morning they came to fetch the colonel. He was calm and serene. He drank a small glass of whiskey. I did not have one myself though I needed it badly. He bowed to me:

"Please tell the King that I'm honored to have served under him."

And he went out into the dawn light.

A fortnight later Learoyd was put aboard a ship bound for England. I could not pass on the Japanese colonel's message, because I was then at Tomani with that old crow Senghir. When Learoyd's ship docked at Colombo, he escaped. He disappeared, and no one ever heard of him again.

In July and August Fergusson attended all the ceremonies marking the reunion of North Borneo with the Crown. In the eyes of everyone, he was the man who had pacified the Murut territory. In September he, too, embarked on a P & O liner bound for England.

I have been told—it is only a rumor—that he had assisted Learoyd's escape.

[254]